# All the Stupid Little Children

Paul McCormack

**Ichabod Dozer Press**

ISBN  978-0-9854620-2-4

Cover: "Creature Choosing Buttock" by John Lurie

*Incidental art from "Learn to Draw: Volume One" by John Lurie. Used by permission, all rights reserved. Buy a copy and be cooler than you are.*

# Table of Contents

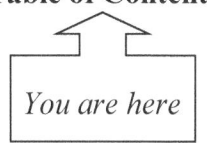

*You are here*

## Acknowledgements:

- Lisa McCool-Grime for her help in editing and compiling this little tome as well as sitting through many a session of lesser works that didn't make the cut.
- John Lurie for lending his art to my little cause and for being an all-around good sport. That and for just generally kicking ass.
- "Word from the Mountain" is dedicated to Kari Wahlgren because she liked it and for being an ear to listen and a wonderfully decent human being.
- Also deserving of mention are Ron Fischer and Rick Watson who somehow managed to keep me trudging down this path. Brent and Adina Premer for being shelter from life's little downpours. Dustin Hansen and Kari Larson for helping me keep all these projects afloat in one capacity or another.

## Forward

"Write another book."

I kept hearing that even though the last one hadn't done much in a financial sense. I'd meant to. I've got half a dozen longer projects still in various stages of completion but admittedly none that's held my interest long enough to polish off.

It might happen someday. This isn't a retirement it's a hiatus. Of course that's what television networks say when something's finished. Let's not dwell.

Let me just say this: poop mullet.

Things were getting too serious there for a moment.

So folks want another book. And I was faced by a very real dilemma: do I actually sit down and endure the freakish marathon of time and energy that a novel requires (they're like children—needy, stupid little children, but you love them anyway) or do I just lump some random crap?

Well, like a true candy ass I chose a combination. The result is this charming little collection you hold in your hand at this very moment. It's a collection of some short stories and sketches and scenes and whatnot. Some were written independently, most were the result of the writer's group I was a part of.

All this to say that despite all of the good intentions and guidance from good people I will still randomly write things like "poop mullet" just because I think it makes me clever. Because nothing says clever more than an outdated hair style made from excrement. Hilarity ensues.

See that? It's hilarity.

So I started putting together this tawdry list of little fictions and started noticing an inordinate number of losers, dogs and underlying themes of disappointment and disillusionment. This is the summary part in case you have to do a report on this for a class. "Disillusionment and disappointment" is critical gold. Of course you will probably have to differentiate the two. Disillusionment is being unhappy with what you have and disappointment is not getting what you want. It's like thermodynamics: you can't win; you can't tie; you can only lose.

But losing is funny. Especially when it's done with flair. This is my advice to all you graduates out there: it will suck, but sometimes it will suck worse for other people and you have to remember to laugh at those people. Laugh hard because tomorrow, well, let's not talk about that.

Where was I? Oh yes, putting a book together. So this is a book and it has a lot of pages, some with more words than others, some with fancier words, some of them are "poop mullet" (hee!) but hopefully they'll make you smile a bit or think a bit or at least look really neat on your coffee table.

*Paul McCormack*
*28.May.2007*

## A Friend Better Than You

Matthew "Dirge" Dergenstein was a toad. That was the current theory at least.

Six months ago Dirge had been unceremoniously dumped on the eve of his one-year anniversary by Tonya, the girl who had the week before dropped several hints that she wanted an engagement ring—soon. Dirge couldn't get another woman to so much as look him in the eyes—or at least look him in the eyes with anything other than contempt.

That was the problem, he figured. There was some sort of secret underground network that kept every woman on the planet informed of all the others comings and goings. That's how they knew things they shouldn't know and how, if you were blacklisted, you were pretty much doomed to a lifetime of celibacy and reheated Spaghetti-O's in your bathrobe with a couple of cats to keep you company. It was a shitty deal and Dirge was on the flushing end of a doozy.

Spence had heard it all before. How Tonya was the only one that Dirge had ever really loved or that the only thing he really missed was how her nose crinkled when she was really truly happy. By the end of month two Spence probably knew every expressive nuance and personal idiosyncrasy of Tonya's better than her own mother did. The difference was Tonya's mother would eternally love and esteem Tonya as life-giver. Spence on the other hand had been largely indifferent to her while she was around and none too sad to see her go when she left.

Thing was, she hadn't left. Every day Dirge would morosely flop down on Spence's couch and talk in depth about a ghost that only he could see, but whom he believed everyone deeply needed to know about. Spence didn't care much if Tonya looked like she was smiling when she slept or about that "special way" she'd curl her toes when she stretched. The only pressing thing Spence wanted to know was when he could get his couch back.

Spence hadn't even known Dirge that well. They had worked together at a furniture store about a year before and while they had been friendly they were in no way close. When Dirge announced he was moving to a new apartment one afternoon and asked his coworkers if any wanted to help, Spence hadn't thought much of it. He showed up an hour or so late to help and discovered he was the only who had actually appeared. Since then Dirge had confused the relief that someone had actually shown up to help carry his couch with a belief that he had a new best friend.

Spence largely ignored him—not picking up the phone when Dirge called if he didn't feel like talking to him, blowing off plans randomly and the like. It wasn't that he hated Dirge; he just didn't find Dirge to be all that interesting. Without fail though, Dirge would still call, happy and optimistic about all things that involved him and Spence. Spence wondered if Dirge actually had little scenarios play out in his head about what great buddies they were—if, in his head, they'd go fishing or hit on twins at the bar or some sort of thing that buddies did in TV shows and beer commercials. The thought that Dirge might have actually considered Spence his sidekick in his little alternate universe wasn't out of the question, either.

In either case, Spence had been able to keep his newfound best friend at a convenient distance for the most part. Every other weekend, if nothing else was going on, Spence would meet Dirge for a drink or they'd hook up for a movie or something largely informal. Dirge thought everything was just peachy and Spence had most of his free time to devote to things he actually cared about. At least until Tonya left.

All of sudden Dirge started showing up on his doorstep at all hours. Sometimes he was drunk, sometimes he was just crying and sometimes he was crying about how drunk he was. At first Spence felt sorry for him and let him pass out on his couch. Unfortunately, Dirge took it as a sign that he had finally found a confidant and a loyal party through his time of trial and tribulation.

It became ritual that Spence would come home from work to find his newest unwanted best friend waiting for him on the landing steps. After that anything Spence would say or do would launch Dirge into a reminiscence or fit of self-pity that he would constantly ask Spence to validate.

It had gotten to the point where Spence would swing by the bottle shop and pick up a case before returning home from work in hopes that Dirge would drink himself into a stupor and leave him with enough time to get some peace and quiet in his own home. In the end, the only thing it really succeeded in doing was increasing Dirge's tolerance level and drawing out his excruciatingly long and aimless reflections on life without love.

Now usually these things fade over time. Self-pity and the pain, no matter how fervently clutched by the bearer, dissipate. The immediacy of the insult and lingering of the injury both become smaller in retrospect and, even though they remain to be a favorite topic of discussion, the topic can at least be changed. But it had been six straight months of Dirge's drunken weeping fits in the living room at three in the morning when Spence had to work the next morning. Spence wasn't even really sure what it felt like to sit on his own couch anymore, as it had become Dirge's official place of moping.

Spence had tried to tell Dirge not to come back. He had changed his phone number and the locks on the door, but it hadn't mattered—Dirge never really called anymore and every day after work he'd be sitting by Spence's front door crying and would trot on in after the door was opened. There wasn't a waking moment where Spence wasn't at work that somehow didn't involve Dirge. The living room started to have the lingering scent of feet and stale beer. It was intolerable.

Dirge would sit, crying at Spence—who would often be in another room in an attempt to reinforce that he was uninterested in the epic tragedy that was Dirge's love life, but to no avail.  He could almost tell what time it was by the comments.  At ten o'clock it was "I just want her to be happy."  At eleven it was "We were so happy together—what could have happened?"  By midnight the self-loathing had kicked in with "How could I have thought she could've loved someone like me?"  At one it was "I wish I had never been born" and the rest of the night usually ended up being incoherent mumbles and wails.

It was a cool fall evening when Spence finally had enough.  He dropped a couple of sleeping pills into Dirge's open beer and waited for them to kick in.  An hour later Dirge was prematurely unconscious, spread out in a frozen flail on the couch.  Spence quickly set to work grabbing the gas can from his truck and splashing it throughout the apartment, with special attention to the living room.  Spence grabbed a couple of items he figured they'd allow him to keep in his jail cell and grabbed Dirge's lighter from the coffee table.  As he glanced across the coffee table he found himself staring directly into Dirge's glassy dilated eyes.

He managed to flop an unsteady arm onto Spence's, grab his hand and give it a little squeeze.

"I could have been a better friend than you.  I would have been better," he mumbled before rolling back over on his side and going back to sleep.

Spence slowly recoiled his hand as Dirge nestled into the couch cushions.  He wasn't sure what to say or how to react.  He wasn't even sure what it had meant.

Later, as he leaned against the police cruiser watching the

brilliant light from the flames and the gently dancing, cascading embers, Spence wondered if he should have called Tonya to tell her what had happened. It was too late now anyway, he thought to himself.

**God in the Aisle**

I met God.

No, really.

Not in some mystical "vision of white and glory" kinda way, either.

I'm serious.

I don't think I'm Elvis and I don't wear tin foil on my head to keep the aliens from controlling my brain. They control my brain better than I do, anyway.

That last thing was a joke. Okay, maybe ill- timed, but it's funny, right?

It's like this: I got a temp job working at a warehouse in the run-down part of town. You know, the part that if you're a tall, skinny, white guy you'd better keep to yourself and not go out after dark? Yeah, that's where it was.

As temps go, it wasn't a horrible gig. I was assigned to work there for two weeks while someone was on vacation or on medical leave or whatever it was. After a while it really doesn't matter why you're there, you show up and they try to ignore you and you get paid and then it's over and you move on to the next thing. Come to think of it, it sounds a lot like prostitution. Nevermind.

Anyway, I was supposed to help maintain various records and invoices in the interim. When I arrived that first Monday morning, I started looking for instructions. After an hour of fruitless searching, I found the site manager. I asked him where my instructions were.

"What instructions?"

"The directions about what I'm supposed to be doing with the paperwork."

"You only have to know two things: Invoices go in the green envelope, requisitions in the manila envelope and only authorized personnel are allowed to handle the invoices, requisitions and the envelopes."

"Am I authorized?"

"No."

"So what should I do?"

"I taped the envelopes to your door so employees can put the forms in the appropriate one."

"So should I send them off everyday?"

8

"No, you're not authorized to handle the envelopes."

"Shouldn't they be sealed or something or at least taken down when no one's around?"

"Probably. I guess I'll do it."

"Because I'm not authorized to handle the envelopes?"

"Exactly."

"So what am I supposed to do since I'm not allowed to handle the paperwork I'm responsible for filing?"

"Um, I dunno. Do you make coffee?"

"Uh, yeah. Do you want some?"

"No, we don't drink coffee on this shift..."

And there it was. I had no purpose whatsoever, but couldn't leave for fear of being fired. So I sat in the little office for the rest of the day. I wrote a letter to my grandmother and put together a grocery list and then sat staring at the flecked tiling on the floor. I suddenly flashed back to detention in high school. It all felt unnervingly similar.

My one diversion was a single drawer in the desk that hadn't been cleaned out. There were seventy-eight unsharpened pencils with the company name monogrammed on the side. I remembered how I'd passed the time in high school.

By the time lunch rolled around, I had gotten 30 pencils stuck in a single overhead panel. I was a little rusty, but I figured that I'd probably be able to get most of the pencils stuck in one panel given enough time.

Two weeks was probably more than enough time.

At lunch I headed to the break room to mingle with my co-workers. Upon entering I realized that not only was I the only temp in the building, but I was the only one who wasn't wearing dusty jeans, a well-worn t-shirts and a flannel. I was their anti-Christ—a white-collar temp who was getting a better hourly wage and whose responsibility was to do exactly nothing while they were supposed to pick up the slack. Apparently word about my unique position had spread quickly and I was dubbed "the Freeloader."

I returned to the little office and resumed my pencil project. Four and a half agonizing hours later with nearly fifty pencils hanging from various ceiling tiles, I gathered my few belongings and went home. As I got into my little hatchback and started back to the freeway, I noticed a little mom-and-pop grocery store about half a block from the warehouse. It was run-down and dingy, but unlike everything else on the street, it looked as if it might actually be open. It seemed a little odd that a little grocery like that would survive when everything else had failed—especially since there didn't seem to be a residential area or major road anywhere nearby. I found my exit and hoped that there was still one cold beer left in the fridge.

Seven rolled around much too soon and I again found myself grasping my styrofoam cup of coffee and maneuvering my Citation through the river of other vehicles collectively chugging towards employment. I actually made decent time and arrived five minutes early. My post-lunch marathon of inactivity filled me with dread. Instead of bustling in early, I decided to check out the little grocery store hoping that I'd be able to find something to waste my time with.

The florescent lighting seemed lacking. There was a slightly off-putting bluish glow that the lights cast. The shadows seemed longer and darker. The tiles on the floor were so old and worn that they looked permanently dirty. It took my eyes a second to adjust to the strange lighting and then I looked around a bit. There was an old cash register to the right with a clear candy display on the side. Behind the counter were a few pictures and framed newspaper clippings although, off-hand, none of them appeared to have anything to do with the store.

"Watch your step, now. I just finished mopping up right there."

An older man stood there looking me over, mop still in hand, peering around the furthest of the five aisles. His face wasn't particularly wrinkled until you reached his forehead, which seemed to collect layers of emotional sediment beginning just above his eyebrows. His dark skin glistened lightly as he wiped his forehead. His eyes had a quiet and tired irritability about them. His hair was neatly trimmed and the white seemed to be completing its victory over the remaining black hair he had left.

"What?" he asked. I'd been staring for some reason.

"Um, do you have any donuts?"

"All that stuff is in the snack aisle," he replied, pointing to the second aisle.

I nodded and promptly slipped.

I felt my face flush red as I scrambled back to my feet. The old man gave an exasperated sigh and looked me over. To my side was a large milky brown pool where my coffee had unceremoniously landed.

"Now I told you to be careful, didn't I? Every day it's the same thing, people come on in, make a mess and then I'm left to clean it up and then they complain that there ain't no service because I'm not behind the counter every second."

"I-I'm, sorry," I sputtered as I realized that not all of my coffee had hit the floor, but had instead left a socially problematic wet spot on the front of my pants. I heard a quiet giggle just over my shoulder but only caught a glimpse of a very pale-skinned black woman out of the corner of my eye.

"Don't pay Selima any mind. She's always about here and there. There's some paper towels behind the counter. You can clean up a little with that. Your donuts are down that aisle, and for goodness sakes, watch where you're going," the man muttered as he began to mop up my coffee.

"Every day it's the same thing. They think they don't have to listen and that I don't know what's going on, but that'll change. The boy'll be back soon and then it'll all be different. No more of this always cleanin' up and

12

complainin' from everyone who comes through that door," he continued to himself.

I quickly and quietly gathered my mini-donuts from the aisle and made my way back the cash register. The old man was still mopping. "Just leave your money on the counter, there. I'll know if you left enough."

I thought it was odd, but counted out the change and laid it on the counter. "That's too much. No tax on food items," the old man said matter-of-factly, his eyes never leaving his mopping. I gathered up a nickel from the pile of loose change.

"If you're looking for something to use it on, there's a little jar by the register for that girl with leukemia."

At that point I could hardly keep the nickel without looking like a total asshole, so I dropped it through the little slot. It landed with tinny plop inside.

"You have yourself a nice day, now, and I'll see you around lunchtime," he said, still engrossed in his mopping.

I shuffled out of the store. Something had felt very odd about the whole experience. I noticed I was running a couple minutes late now—not that it really mattered. I tried to slip into the building unnoticed. I was largely successful, catching only a few nasty glances as I crept towards the office. With a good day's worth of practice under my belt I'd probably be able to get upwards of forty pencils today in one tile. I slipped into my office and was instantly horrified.

The floor was covered in plastic, the desk was draped in a tarp and overhead all the ceiling tiles had been removed leaving only a skeletal support frame with once-hidden ductwork and pipes exposed.

The door opened behind me and the site manager entered, accompanied by a couple of guys in paint-stained coveralls. He looked at me, as if surprised to see me.

"Oh, you're here. Listen; since the office is open there was some remodeling we were going to do anyway. I figured since you really didn't have anything to do, it wouldn't matter if you could not do it in the office."

"Um, so where am I supposed to, um, work?"

"Hell, I don't even know what you're supposed to be doing, shooter. Sit in the breakroom all day for all I care."

"So I'm not fired?"

"Fired? Listen, regulations state that we need an administrative staff member available on site at all times. I can't afford to have you not not working here right now."

"Why is an administrative staff person required on staff?"

"In case of a problem with the invoices or requisitions or the filing of the envelopes."

"Which I'm not authorized to handle."

"Right."

"Okay, so I'm supposed to be available to not work in case of emergency at which point I'll be allowed not to handle the invoices, requisitions or their respective envelopes."

"Yup."

"So, under those special circumstances, what would happen if there was an emergency with the paperwork that I'm not allowed handle?"

"You'll be put on suspension immediately pending an inquiry at which point it'll be determined that you were negligent in your duties regarding the invoices, requisitions and envelopes—"

"Even if those duties include not handling the paperwork because I'm not authorized to do so?"

"Even if those duties include not handling the paperwork because you're not authorized to do so. At that time your employment status will be re-evaluated and you'll likely be terminated with a negative recommendation."

"Because I didn't do what I wasn't supposed to do when I was not supposed to do it?"

"That about says it."

"...You say I can sit in the break room all day?"

"Well, yeah, but the guys don't seem to like you very much. You might be better off just wandering around or something."

"Do I need to stay on site?"

"Well, if you leave and there's an emergency, you'll be fired."

"And if I stay and there's an emergency?"

"You'll be fired for not doing your job in an emergency."

"Because I'm not allowed to handle the paperwork."

"Yes, I've gone over all this already."

"Just making sure."

The site manager looked me over and shook his head as he left the office and headed down the hallway. "Damn temps," he muttered under his breath.

I spent the next three uneasy hours sitting in the break room, trying not to make direct eye contact with anyone. Most of them didn't seem to care, although my presence appeared to be a bit of an irritation to some. There are points in a temping career where the absurdity of life comes rushing up to meet you in a deluge of indifferent fury. I was having one of those moments. Not only was I unable to do anything, let alone anything resembling my job description, but my place of sanctuary and my sole pastime were also usurped in one fell stroke. As I considered buying another pack of cheese crackers from the break room snack machine, I found myself thinking about the little grocery store some more.

I couldn't place the feeling I'd had in the store specifically. It was familiar, but from a long time ago. I was pretty sure it was a good feeling, although it wasn't a normal kind of good. It was as if everything was operating on all sorts of different levels in there. I sighed and looked at the clock. It was almost eleven thirty. It was early yet for lunch, but it wasn't as if I had anything pressing to do. I gathered up my cheese crackers and my half-empty cup of coffee and skulked out of the building, back to the grocery store.

"A little early for a lunch," was my greeting as I shuffled in.

"Uh, I guess. Things were slow..."

"You don't have to explain nothin' to me," he said, never looking up from his magazine behind the counter. "Just making an observation's all."

I glanced around trying to catch a glimpse of the pale woman I had seen earlier, but there was no sign of her. I began half-heartedly browsing. The selection was pretty run-of-the-mill. Prices weren't bad, but I really didn't have cause to take advantage of the special on a dozen eggs or the two-for-one coupon offer on the bottle of curry. The bell above the front door rang. I watched curiously as a large black woman came in. The man behind the counter's expression changed and he smiled widely.

"Well, Mrs. Jackson good to see you again. Early today, I see."

She beamed with an infectiously large smile, "Now you ol' trickster, you knew full well I'd be dropping by today and that I'd be coming with good news. You can't fool me with those innocent eyes you've got there."

The man at the counter chuckled. "Well, what I know is that daughter of yours better work hard. A full academic scholarship don't come easy."

"Well, I just came by to thank you for all you done for us. There's not a day that goes by that I don't tell Lisha how lucky we are that—"

He patted her hand as if to indicate something was different. She looked over her shoulder to see me poorly trying to conceal my interest by looking through the canned goods. She looked back at the old man and whispered, "That's not—?"

"No, no. He's just dropping by for a little bit. Just a regular customer. The kind we need to keep a little place like this runnin'. Now you go ahead and pick up one of those frozen pies you like so much and you tell Lisha congratulations for me, alright?"

Mrs. Jackson smiled again and grasped his hand. "Thank you so much, for everything." She looked as if she were going to cry.

"Now, now, no need for all of that. There's still a lot more hard work comin' for all of you. Now you go and bake up that pie and have yourself a nice evenin' on me."

Out of the corner of my eye I saw sudden movement. I turned my head and managed to see the pale woman disappearing behind the swinging double doors that lead back into what I guessed was the refrigerated storage area.

"She's a quick one, isn't she?" said the old man behind the counter with a smirk. "I tried to tell you before that you wouldn't see her, didn't I? Selima's hard to pin down, but you can always tell she's there," he chuckled.

I looked around, bewildered. There was definitely something strange going on here, but I couldn't exactly place it.

"You gonna poke around all day or are you plannin' on buyin' somethin'?" he asked with a mock gruffness.

I reluctantly grabbed a snack bag of chips and made my way to the counter.

"That be all for ya?" he asked. I nodded.

The bell at the door rang again and in strode a nun. She was elderly with wrinkles and wispy white hair but disarmingly spry. She shot the man at the counter a haughty look. The old man just nodded warily and said, "Good day, ma'am." She smiled with an air of contempt and nodded.

I realized that I had wanted to grab a cherry soda and went around to the coolers. As I retrieved the bottle, I looked over to see the nun slipping a handful of candy bars into her pocket. She glanced over and saw me but instead of looking shocked or embarrassed, she winked and flashed a smile. She then strode back to the front of the store.

"I'm afraid your selection is quite poor. I'll have to go somewhere else to find what I need," she said irritably and walked out.

I was amazed. I'd seen people try to steal things a couple times, but never with such brashness in the face of being caught. I brought my drink to the counter. "Hey, I don't mean to bother you, but that nun just stole, like, five candy bars," I whispered, feeling guiltily to be narcing on a nun.

"Yeah, I know. Not much happens here that I don't know about. They come in; they steal and they think I don't notice it, but I do. There'll be a reckoning one day, don't you worry about that. When my boy comes back everything thought unseen will be revealed." He let out a tried sigh and looked at the door for a moment. "That'll be $2.75," he muttered.

I spent the rest of the day waiting for my non-duties to come to an end, all the while trying to keep from being underfoot since the rest of the staff already didn't like me. The site manager had begun just calling me "Freeloader" to my face and wasn't especially helpful about what I could be doing. Nevertheless, I waited dutifully until five o'clock and then punched out.

As I made my way to the car I was already beginning to dread the next eight days I'd have to spend hiding in corners and being ridiculed for nothing more than just being present. I sighed and began the trip home.

The answer came to me in a dream. It was the one where I was back in high school and Mindy Lasowski, the girl I secretly had a crush on all the way through Geometry junior year, had asked me to meet her in the art room. Of course, I couldn't find the art room and the harder I looked the later it got. So I'm wandering the halls and I can't find anything until I run across Dusty Gabornick who was the creepy old guy I knew in college who tells me "It's up to God! Everything's up to God!"

After that there was some thing with a poodle and me being naked in front of my geography class, but I got the message. I'd walked into some strange metaphor for the universe, except instead of just being a metaphor, God was actually running the store! I tried to unravel the various philosophical and theological implications of God running a grocery store, but I fell asleep and dreamed about being naked in high school again.

In the morning I was understandably wary of the epiphany I'd had the night before, but as I mulled it over it seemed at least somewhat probable. Well, maybe not probable, but it was an interesting enough theory to at least amuse myself with for a while. I walked into work and punched in, avoiding the stares of the other workers. I strode in, bound and determined, right back out the front door and promptly ran into the site manager.

"What's the rush, Freeloader?"

"I'm going to the grocery store."

"Couldn't do that before you punched in?"

"Well, if I hadn't, then I wouldn't have been logged as being on-site."

"But you're leaving the site."

"Yeah."

"But you could be fired."

"Yeah."

"Don't you have any pride in what you do?"

"On the contrary, I have nothing but the deepest sense of duty and pride in knowing that I'm not doing the best job I can't do."

"Um."

"What's more, I bet if you think about it, I don't do this job better than any other temp you've ever had before. The fact that I can not do my job from the grocery store as well as I don't do it from the work site itself is impressive, don't you think? I mean, have you ever seen anyone not do their job better than me from a completely different building?"

"I'm going to have to make mention of this in your personnel file," the site manager intoned gravely.

"Wonderful. Make sure to note that I'm clearly performing my allotted duties insofar that I'm not violating company policies by performing my allotted duties. Also make note that I report early to make sure that there's nothing more that I can't do. You know, if this all works out, maybe I'll get on as a full-time, regular employee and then I can not do things for you all the time," I replied happily.

The site manager looked at me through furrowed brow and then shook his head and walked in the building. "Damn wise-ass college-boy temps," he grumbled. I felt a strange sense of accomplishment from articulating my own situation and managing to frustrate someone other than myself with it.

I walked through the doors of the grocery store with all the confidence in the world. Behind the counter the old man looked over his bifocals with an air of skepticism. "Well, hello again. Looks like someone ate their Wheaties this mornin'. If you're lookin' for coffee, I just put a pot on."

I nodded and began browsing the aisles. I felt free. I wasn't planning on going back to work, at least not for a while. I had my theory on the grocery store that interested me and I was getting paid to figure it out. I grabbed a small box of graham crackers, a bottle of Yoo-Hoo and a couple sticks of beef jerky. I marched over the counter and laid them out. The old man took to punching the keys on the old style cash register. I paid in full and then leaned on the counter, watching the old man.

He looked at me quizzically. "Somethin' wrong?"

"Not at all," I smiled.

"What? I got something on my face?" he asked running his hand by his mouth and nose.

"No, you're fine."

"Boy, if you're messin' with me—"

"No, I just like it here.  Do you think I can stay?"

"What?  Is there somethin' wrong with you, son?  You hit your head or something?"

I looked around before leaning in and whispered to him, "I got you figured out."

A look of mild surprise and annoyance crept across his eyes as he peered over his glasses.  "Is that so?  Well then, that changes everything doesn't it?  I mean, if you got a grocer figured out, the whole world is your oyster, now isn't it?" he grumbled as he went back to reading a newspaper that had been folded neatly on the other side of the cash register.

I smiled and nodded, playing along.  "No, no, of course, I understand.  I don't know anything.  Not a thing.  Honest."

The old man didn't look up from his paper and just nodded with a disinterested "Mm-hm."

The bell behind me rang and I glimpsed over my shoulder to see a well-dressed businessman punch through the front door like a force of nature.  He blindly gestured towards the old man and me in some kind of greeting and headed straight to the rear of the store.  He was talking loudly and angrily on a cell phone about buying and selling and options and who knows what else.  I never had much use for the lingo of money primarily because ignorance of it kept me from being interesting to money folk.

I watched him as he nonchalantly sorted through various things in the cooler and the rear racks. I turned back to the old man whose eyes hadn't left his newspaper.

"Funny thing, newspapers," he said, as if he were simply musing to himself. "They'll tell ya what's happened, near as they can at least, and everyone is so interested. They can find out what their favorite popstar had for lunch and who they lied to while they were there. Thing is, they can't tell what's happening now. They can speculate, but what good is speculation, really?

"Now, if it were a perfect world you could look at a newspaper and see what was going on right then. You could read that your wife was cheating on you or that your grandma was dying or any other type of sordid thing that interests people. Why do you think that is?"

"Um, why what is?"

"I thought you had it all figured out," he answered wryly from his newspaper. In the back I could still hear the sharply dressed suit rambling on and on. "Why is it that people seem to be drawn to the most horrible aspects of each other?"

I immediately thought I was being tested or being given some sort of parable. I just shrugged and waited to be enlightened. The loud cell man stormed out of the store, still screaming on his cell phone, a jug of milk under one arm and a bag of nacho chips under the other.

"Of course I probably wouldn't read it anymore. As it is, it's just a minor distraction I use to pass the time. Besides,

I don't need a newspaper to tell that guy just left without paying," he sighed.

I waited patiently for him to answer his own question. After a couple of minutes he hadn't said anything and had begun the crossword puzzle.

"So, um, what's the answer?" I ventured.

"Well, let's see, it's an eleven-letter word that means 'dazzling appearance.' Third letter is 's" and fourth should be a 'p.'"

I chuckled. He was trying to bait me. He was clever.

"I wasn't talking about that."

"Well, Mr. Got-it-all-Figured, why don't you tell me, then."

It *was* a challenge. I thought for a moment; I didn't want to come off as dense, but in situations like this it was almost inevitable. Best to stink to the basics, I decided.

"Well, this is all my opinion, of course." Good, begin with a disclaimer. Very safe. "But I guess there's an element of depravity that we all feed off of. I mean that's the whole thing, right? We're not supposed to be good are we? I mean, we're *supposed* to be good, but it's just not in us. We're rotten and only trying to please ourselves regardless of who gets in the way; at least that's the theory, right? So I suppose part of us knows that we're no good and so we like to look at the horrible things other people are doing so we can say 'Well, at least I'd never do *that*.' Of course that's just a theory."

Waiting. He didn't move or look at me or anything else other than his crossword for a full fifteen seconds. Then a slight smile crossed his lips and he glanced up at me.

"You know what I think?"

"What?"

"I think the word's 'resplendent.'" And with a self-satisfied little chuckle he scribbled the word into the puzzle.

"You don't make it very easy to know you, do you?" I asked with just a hint of frustration.

Again his eyes never left his crossword. "Why should I make it something it's not? I don't make it easy to know me because knowing me isn't easy. All your generation wants is something quick, accessible and easy. When was the last time you actually sat down and did something the long way because it's better that way? It's all drive-thrus and e-mails and cell phones nowadays. Knowing someone isn't something you do in fifteen minutes while you're on a coffee break, and I ain't one to act like it is."

After a moment's pause he looked up at me, "Feel better now?"

"Not really."

"Figured as much. I don't suppose there's much chance that you're going back to your job so I can do mine, is there?"

"I'd rather not."

"Fine then, but you ain't gonna just stand there. If you got your heart set on hidin' out here, then you won't just be taking up my counter space, understand?"

I nodded.

"There's the broom," he pointed off at the end of the aisle by a pair of swinging double doors where a beaten and worn broom was tilted against the corner of the walls.

"And don't go through the doors," the old man warned sternly.

"Why? What's behind the doors?" Had I stumbled on the gate to heaven or a modern-day tree of the knowledge of good and evil?

"Just stock, but OSHA and my insurance say no one but staff can go back there. And you ain't staff."

I grabbed the broom and began pushing it around, watching the old man to see if he'd give up some sort of clue about his purpose here or accidentally reveal some great, hidden, universal truth.

After a few minutes he sighed and looked me dead in the eyes. "Do I smell funny?"

"Um, no."

"Well, do I got some ink all over my face?"

"No."

"Does my appearance in any way suggest to you that I might be in some way dirty, pungent or otherwise ill-kempt?"

"No."

"Then pay attention to the floor cuz that's what needs to be cleaned. You ain't getting' a thing accomplished by lookin' at somethin' other than what you're supposed to be doin'."

I was surprised at the force of his irritation, but it began to settle in. I began sweeping in earnest. This was going to be one of those "Kung-Fu" kind of student-teacher things. He'd say something cryptic and then make me do something until I figured out what metaphor I was acting out. Was that "Kung-Fu"? Maybe it was "The Karate Kid." It didn't matter, anyway.

Determined to be a good disciple, I worked hard and without interruption for the whole day. A few people came in, including Mrs. Jackson who was as bright and sociable as ever to the old man, but when she saw me, a look of disbelief crossed her face. She looked questioningly at the old man who just shrugged and then pointed out that I'd missed a spot in polishing the stainless steel refrigerated cooler doors.

Other than Mrs. Jackson, the other patrons of the little grocery all seemed strange. I saw most of them steal, but there was something about them—about *all* of them that seemed, well, the same. I thought it over and I couldn't quite put my finger on it. As five o'clock rolled around, I finished scrubbing the well -worn tile floor and headed back to the warehouse to punch out. As I walked out the door, the old man was standing there, flipping through some old receipts and papers. Next to him was the girl. She flashed an elfin grin, but didn't rush into the shadows this time. She gave me a little half wave as I reached for the door.

"I s'pose you'll be lookin' to come back tomorrow, too?" sighed the old man.

"Um, yeah, I guess."

"Well, I guess then tomorrow I'll have you help Selima strip and wax the floor."

"Um, okay."

"You have a good day, now."

It was the first semi-nice thing the old man had said to me the whole day. I walked over to the warehouse, punched out and headed to my car. I now had a few things to puzzle over. What was the great universal truth I was supposed to figure out? Was I supposed to figure it out or would be it one of those things where I deny him three times before I can understand? And what was up with the visitors to the store? Mrs. Jackson seemed okay, but the others—there were other forces at work, I was sure of that much.

I was still mulling over things as I shuffled into my apartment. I tossed my keys onto the cluttered table and considered that I'd either have to do dishes or order out... again. I'd already had pizza the last three days. Maybe Thai? As I was holding the phone, having a silent, dialectical debate over the merits of food delivered in cardboard boxes versus little paper buckets, it sprung to life giving off a piercing warble. I was caught a little off-guard. I answered the phone with a tentative "hullo."

"Hello?" came the nasally response.

"Hello?"

"...Hello?"

"Gramma, how are you?"

"...Hello?"

"Gramma?"

"Yes?"

"Hi Gramma."

"Hello?"

""Yes Gramma, I'm here. How are you?"

"Are you there?"

"Yes Gramma, how have you been?"

"Oh, hi. I've been doing alright. How are you?"

"I'm doing fine, Gramma."

"What?"

"Turn up your hearing aid, Gramma."

"…Hold on, I'm going to turn up my hearing aid," there was a pause and then a high-pitched hollow whistle that dipped and quickly rose in pitch. Then another pause.

"…Hello?"

"Yeah, Gramma, I'm here."

"Oh, hello. I thought I'd call and say hello."

"Well, I'm glad you did."

"Yes… So how are you doing?"

"Things are going fine, Gramma. I've been—"

"You say things are going fine?"

"Yes, things are fine, Gramma. I've been working pretty steady lately."

"Oh that's good. Are you still at that office building?"

"No, that was a while ago.  I work for a company that has me fill-in for other people when they're sick or on vacation."

"Oh, I see…  How is Meghan?"

"Meghan's married, Gramma.  We broke up a long time ago, remember?  She sent you an invitation to her wedding."

"Oh that's right, that's right.  She was nice, wasn't she?  Have you talked to her lately?"

"Not since the officer dropped off the paper saying I couldn't call her anymore."

A sudden whistling interrupted the line.

"Hold on," more whistling of varying pitches and then silence.

"I clipped the article."

"What article?"

"The wedding announcement.  I sent it to her; I thought she might want a copy."

"That was nice of you, Gramma."

"So where are you working now?"

"I'm filling in at a warehouse."

"Oh, isn't that something?  What do you do?"

"Nothing."

"What?"

"Nothing."

"…Do you enjoy what you're doing?"

"Sure.  It pays the bills."

"That's so important.  I see in the paper that no one can find jobs anymore.  It's good to have a job."

"Yes, it's nice."

"Do you think you'd like to keep doing what you're doing now?"

"Um, I guess.  I'm not sure if I could find someone to pay for it, though."

"Uh-huh…  So have you made any friends at your job?"

"Well, I met some interesting people, actually.  Funny you should ask, I think I met God."

"Is that so?  Maybe you two could go have dinner sometime and keep on after you finish there."

"Um, I guess I could ask."

"You know I met your grandfather at the diner I worked at. He ordered a sandwich and I served it to him."

"Yeah, you've told me about that—" more whistling.

"…I'm sorry," whistling trembled then ceased. "Well, it's nice to hear you're making friends at your work."

"Yeah, it's kinda weird, I guess. I mean, it *is* God."

"I met Lawrence Welk once when I was younger. Real nice man—" there was a knock in the background and then silence for a second. I heard some indistinguishable conversation in the background and then a rustling on the phone.

"I have to go. Lula's here to do my hair."

"Okay, thanks for calling."

"Okay, you go have fun with Todd and I'll talk to you later."

"Todd—?"

Click.

Well, it had been a first step. It was probably a pretty ineffectual step since my grandmother would be telling everyone about my new friend, Todd, but I'd told someone about what was going on. It hadn't sounded crazy when I'd said it, either. I could feel my own confidence in my conclusions growing. I grabbed a cold beer out of the fridge and dialed up the Bangkok Express to order my dinner.

I flipped through the channels on the television. When was it that all the shows became lesser versions of other shows? They were all the same—same jokes, same sarcasm, same opening music, same interchangeable pretty-person casts. I flipped to a news channel, which wasn't the same—they hadn't thought to put a laugh track with the news, at least not yet.

I recognized the man beaming into the camera as he was introduced by the interviewer—it was the loud businessman who hadn't paid for his things earlier. As part of the introduction, the interviewer began to list his credits and, suddenly, I had a revelation—this person was responsible directly or indirectly for most of the programs on television. There was a reason they all seemed the same, because they were all the products of the same milquetoast mind. And then it all clicked.

The old man *was* God. Selima, the pale woman, was the Holy Ghost. They were waiting for the "Son" to come back and set everything right. And every snarly, brazen, smug non-paying shoplifter was none other than the Devil himself. He took on all these forms to try and cover up what God could always tell—that he was around and being a pain in the ass. Mrs. Jackson, well, she was probably just Mrs. Jackson.

I reflected on the shoplifters—they looked like they had no reason to steal. They should have been able to either get what they wanted or should have had too much to lose to do it, but the nun had just grinned when she was caught and the suit hadn't cared if anyone noticed. Maybe that was what I was supposed to do—stop the Devil from stealing. But it seemed like if God had wanted the Devil to stop swiping Ho-ho's or Snickers bars or whatever else the Devil would try to take, that He could just make him not steal. He could probably ban him from the store, while He was at it. I didn't feel up to the task of banishing the Dark Lord of Hell from the store if God himself didn't seem to be concerned with his presence.

As the security call button whined irritably to me, indicating my dinner had arrived, I figured I almost had it all worked out, but I'd need a little more time.

My novelty had worn off at the warehouse. The only real difference was that I'd become "The Fuckin' Freeloader" instead of just "Freeloader," but all-in-all, they had come to tolerate me—which was easier since I only punched in and then went straight to the grocery store. The Old Man didn't even bemoan my presence anymore; he'd just gesture towards a mop bucket, broom or some other tool of the janitorial field and went back to his crossword.

Most of the time I was assigned to help Selima. She was always warm and friendly, but never said a word. The only sound I got out of her was the occasional giggle when I did something she found to be foolish, like when the floor buffer got away from me. Where the Old Man feigned indifference, Selima was always the first to grab a glass of water or a candy bar for me. With snack from the store she'd hand them to me and then bring her finger to her lips in false secrecy, as if the Old Man wasn't supposed to know. Most of the time, I saw Him stealing a glance at us and shaking His head. He never said anything and I caught him chuckling to himself at Selima's playful faux-attempts to sneak something by Him. In all fairness, it was kind of strange.

I'd been brought up with the good ol' fashioned Protestant "three as one" idea of God. The fact that the Son was nowhere to be found was a little strange, although I'm sure you could find some sort of justification for it, but the mock antagonism and benevolent ribbing between Selima and the Old Man sent me for a loop. If they were all the same entity, shouldn't they be doing something more, well, deity-like instead of playing little peek-a-boo games with each other? Perhaps the distinction required there to be some tension or conflict, however good-natured it was for them to be separate. A throbbing began in my head and I finally realized why I got a D in my intro to philosophy class.

I was running an ancient buffer over the worn tile floor when Mrs. Jackson entered the store. She'd grown accustomed to me and would just give me a quick nod in acknowledgment before wandering around for her shopping or going over to talk to the old man. That day she gathered a loaf of bread and a box of breakfast cereal before sauntering over to the counter. I couldn't hear anything over the buffer, but the conversation didn't seem particularly in-depth.

I stopped buffing for a moment to wipe the thin sheen of sweat from my forehead. Selima was paging through the pages of a beauty magazine by the magazine rack, disinterested in my progress. The little bell above the door rang and all eyes turned to the door. In skipped a doe-eyed, blonde girl of five or six. She wore a fancy, white dress and had a light blue ribbon in her hair. She flashed an adorable, little smile to all of us and proceeded to skip towards the back of the store. She was pure evil.

I looked around at the others. Mrs. Jackson stood appalled, watching the child, while Selima nibbled at her thumbnail anxiously. The Old Man sighed and shook his head. There wasn't a sound in the entire store aside from the little girl's humming and her feet clicking happily on the tile floor. We all waited to see what would happen. Occasionally I could see the girl peering around the end of the shelving units and giggling at us, but she didn't stay in sight long and I never got much of a look beyond the top of her head.

After a few minutes she came skipping back down the aisle. Her dress was grotesquely stretched and bulging all over. Around the sleeves and collar, edges of various bags, candy bars and Lord knows what else were showing. She smiled at all of us and did a little wave as she headed for the door. With each step her clothes made crinkling and crunching noises as her pilfered treasures shifted and settled underneath her clothes. I was amazed—the other thefts had been brazen, but this was absurd. Even Selima's expression was one of sheer disbelief. Mrs. Jackson was horrified and looked at the Old Man pleadingly.

"Excuse me there, missy," the Old Man intoned with a meticulously measured rhythm.

The little girl smiled but continued for the door.

"I said, excuse me there," the Old Man said, a deeper rumble starting to rise in his voice.

The little girl didn't even acknowledge that he had said anything and tugged at the door.

And it didn't move.

She pulled again, more forcefully, and then rattled at it, trying to get it to budge.

"Enough!" the Old Man exploded.

The little girl looked at him exasperated. "What!?!"

The Old Man didn't move from behind the counter, but this time his eyes weren't set on his crossword. They were singularly focused on the little girl. A mocking grin slowly curled her lips.

"I'm gonna tell my mom you were mean to me and then she's gonna call my dad and then you'll be in big trouble."

The Old Man looked her over for a second. "My boy's coming back soon."

"So? I don't care. My mom's just outside and she's gonna be—"

"You didn't let me finish," the Old Man growled with the first menace I'd heard from Him. "My boy's coming back soon, and he'll take care of all the problems I've been having 'round here. But make no mistake, missy, I may be old, but I still have salt enough to give you a lickin'."

The little girl's expression had changed. Gone was the confident arrogance and in its place was the look of someone clearly shaken.  Just when I thought the tide had turned, I saw that glint in her eye and suddenly her eyes welled with tears.  A wail of wounded pride and insubordinate fury pierced the air.  The little girl stomped her feet and let out angry howls of indignation at everyone present.  When no one appeared moved by her outburst she threw herself to the floor and began kicking her legs and flailing her arms.  Snacks and candy began to whip out of her overstuffed dress as her tantrum continued.

After five minutes she lay on the ground, whimpering and sobbing.  The Old Man stood behind the counter, arms crossed, a look of irritation on his face.

"You done now?"

She let out a shriek as a reply.

"Well, you take as long as you need.  I got all day."

Her eyes met his eyes and there was silence.  She stood up slowly and brushed her dress off nonchalantly; at her feet was a small pile of the items that had been stuffed inside her dress.  She gave a quick sneer in His direction and walked to the door and pulled on it.  I thought the encounter was over, but the door didn't budge.  She stared at the Old Man with a look of shock and surprise on her face. The Old Man still stood there with his arms crossed.

"What?" the little girl whined.

The Old Man said nothing, but stood unwavering behind the counter.

"This isn't very nice. You should let me go now, I gave it all back."

Nothing.

She looked pleadingly at Mrs. Jackson who seemed to have been caught off-guard.

"You saw, right? Tell him," the girl pleaded.

Mrs. Jackson was unnerved and looked to the Old Man for some sort of response, but He remained motionless and silent behind the counter.

The little girl turned to Selima and me, fear growing in her eyes.

"Please, I won't tell my mom. I just wanna go home. I know I was bad, but I'm sorry."

I was feeling strangely guilty at the girl's tearful petition. I looked to Selima for her reaction. Selima giggled.

The girl's expression changed as soon as she saw Selima's stifled laughter. She let out a disgusted sigh and marched over to the counter, reached in her dress and slapped a skillfully concealed chocolate bar down on the worn top of it.

"There. You can have your stupid candy bar. I hope it makes you happy," she muttered.

"I don't care if you take it," the Old Man replied. "Just pay for it."

42

The little girl took a deep breath as if to unload another tirade when something happened.  The Old Man almost smiled.

It was somewhere between a smirk and a grin, actually, but it was a self-satisfied, triumphant, little expression.  There was no contest.  There had never been a contest.  The Old Man had been playing possum waiting for the right time to show the Devil who was in charge and who had been in charge the entire time.

The little girl made a final sigh of irritation and then reached inside a pocket concealed in the dress and produced a crumpled bill which she threw on the counter.

"You're an asshole," she snarled as she stomped out of the shop, the door now opening freely.

"Yeah, I probably am," sighed the Old Man still grinning.

"The biggest, baddest asshole you're ever likely to meet," He mused contentedly as the door slammed.

"Goodness," Mrs. Jackson exclaimed quietly to no one in particular.

"Now, you don't worry yourself about any of it, Mrs. Jackson.  You know how it goes.  Look at me, do I look worried?"

"No," she sighed.

"Of course not, and if I'm not worried then you shouldn't be getting all riled up either, should you?"

"I know."

"Good, now you go ahead and don't worry about the bread and cereal today and you tell Lisha 'Hi' from me."

"Oh I couldn't—"

"Now I won't have any arguin'. You go ahead and take 'em."

Mrs. Jackson smiled widely and nodded. She looked like she might cry, but she gathered her things and left with a smile.

Selima was gathering the various items the girl had dropped. I took advantage of the lull and went to the counter.

"That was amazing," I chattered excitedly. "I mean when he started kicking and screaming and carrying on—"

"He?"

"Yeah, the little girl."

"So why did you say 'he'?"

"You know why."

"If I knew why, I wouldn't have asked, now would I?"

"Oh come on, you're always doing little things like that. Asking some kind of obtuse question so people can find the metaphor behind it. It's kinda your thing."

"Boy, what in the sam hill are you talking about?"

"You know..." I made a quick sideways glance to make sure no one else was around, "the Devil."

"What?"

"I got it figured out. I worked it all through."

He shook his head. "You're one strange white boy, you know that?"

"You can deny it, but I figured out the metaphor—"

"What is it with you and metaphors? Metaphor for what? You realize how crazy you sound?"

"It's a metaphor for the universe. And you're God and keeping everything going and how the Devil steals and all of it—it's all a metaphor for how things really are. And you had me clean and everything so I'd figure out that we're all responsible for each other and the planet and—"

"I had you clean cuz you were crowding me at my counter. That and the floor was dirty—"

"Dirty with sin!" I exclaimed triumphantly.

"Now listen, you've been a hard worker and all, but my boy's coming soon—"

"Because he's Jesus—"

"No, because he's supposed to be back soon.  And I don't suspect he'll take kindly to all this crazy talk—"

"Because it's a metaphor for extremists, or jihad or—"

"Because he doesn't like crazy talkin' white boys hangin' around the store."

Selima was ignoring us both, wandering around the aisles putting away the nearly stolen goods in their appropriate spaces.

"You can't tell me this isn't some kind of parable—"

"You keep lookin' for every little thing to mean somethin' else.  It ever occur to you that you should do things cuz some things need to be done?  I had you clean up that spill back by the coolers because someone could slip and hurt themselves at worst and at best, it just looks bad.  And I run a good shop.  Been here 38 years before you and the Devil and your metaphors—"

"So you admit that was the Devil?"

"...Alright.  It was the Devil and I'm God and that display case with the Baby Ruths is Richard Nixon and the restroom is Niagara Falls.  There are all your metaphors. Happy?"

I wasn't exactly sure how to interpret the whole outburst, but I nodded. The Old Man shook his head and walked to the back room.

"Selima, this boy's givin' me a headache. Mind the store," and with that, He disappeared into the back.

The rest of the day was quiet. I heard the Old Man sorting things out in the back, but He never returned to the front. I left that day wondering what was in store for the next day. I punched out at the warehouse to the disdainful stares of the other workers there. It didn't matter, I had it all figured out: while they were moving boxes or doing inventory or whatever it was they did, I'd be hanging out with God.

I'd like to say that I knew it was coming. Or maybe that, in retrospect, I've figured out why it all happened the way it did. Maybe it's one of those "mysterious ways" kinda things. In either case the day started out like the ones before. I showered and got dressed. I made my coffee and got the Citation started and began the journey to work. I don't even remember what I was thinking about.

I took the exit to work and got within a block of the warehouse when I was greeted with a temporary road barrier that simply read "Road Closed." I didn't think much of it. I turned around and went a block over to come at it sideways just to find another sign. I drove around for another fifteen minutes and realized that the whole area around the grocery and the warehouse was blocked off. I parked the car and started in by foot. I probably wasn't supposed to be there, but there wasn't anyone around to say I couldn't go. In either case, there was nothing posted about the sidewalk being closed.

As I turned the corner I felt my jaw drop.  Where the warehouse had stood were only a few rouge supports left erect, broken and burned.  They jutted up from the ground, serving as little guideposts around the debris where the warehouse had stood.  I froze as a hand fell on my shoulder.  I whirled around to find myself face to face with the site manager.  He looked tired and disoriented.

"Freeloader, it's you," he murmured.

"What happened?"

"They say it was a gas main.  Took out over a city block.  Just got the fire out a couple hours ago."

"You mean it's all like this?"

He nodded sadly.

"So what are you doing here?" I asked.

He shrugged, "The corporate liaison came out to examine the site... and to fire me..."

"They fired you?"

The site manager broke into tears, "The envelopes... they're gone.  Blown to kingdom come, burned to a crisp and buried under a ton of rubble.  I was going to take the envelopes off the door before I left last night, but I forgot."

I felt sorry for him. Granted, he hadn't been anything but irritable toward me, but it still seemed unfortunate that he'd lost his job.

"And you know what the worst part is? Because it happened after business hours, I can't even write you up for not handling the envelopes in an emergency situation when you weren't supposed to," he sobbed.

"I get fired and you get severance and a letter of recommendation," he wailed.

I patted him on the back as he sobbed between little gasps of "Why me? Why not Freeloader?"

After a few minutes I managed to get him on his way and I went to the grocery store. It was hard to tell where I was exactly; every burned- out husk of a building looked more or less the same. I finally found it, or what was left of it. The only way I managed to find it was by the little bell, still dangling on a broken piece of framework. It rang lightly as a bird bounced up and down on it as a makeshift perch.

It was gone. In a couple days there would be nothing left to distinguish it from anything else that had been there. What was it all supposed to mean?

I stood there in shocked silence and didn't even hear her come up behind me.

"It's a real shame," Mrs. Jackson sighed. "Been coming here for over thirty years and in one night, it's all gone."

"How...?"

"Well, newsman said it was a gas line. Wouldn't doubt it 'round here. Doesn't seem nothin' gets fixed until something bad happens."

"But how could He let it happen?"

"Who?"

"God."

"Well, I don't know. I s'pose in the big picture one lil' ol' grocery store doesn't mean too much—'specially compared to all the wars and such going on. Probably just as well; Safeway's cheaper anyhow. I guess I just got fond of the old place."

"But if He let this happen, what hope is there for any of us?"

Mrs. Jackson looked at me ruefully. "He was right, you are a strange one. Don't worry, I'm sure Selima and him'll be just fine. Besides, his boy is s'posed to be back any day now. Give 'em all a little time to be together instead of having to worry about the store. It'll all work out for the best, don't you worry," she said with a smile as she turned to go.

"But what does it all mean?"

She just laughed as she walked away down the street. "Honey, it don't mean a thing."

## The Confessions of St Mullet

I have incontinence of the mouth. I need to speak but the words won't come, or will come but one drop at a time, relieving next to nothing and only showing how helpless I am. Either that or I just can't stop it—it pours from me, unseemly and reckless. I want to stop, to contain it and eek it out evenly, but I just keep talking and sharing and prying and blabbering.

"I will show you this country," she says with a sly grin. She's flirting because she knows I can't. I can tell her intentions are dishonorable because I have no idea what she's talking about. Which reminds me of a story:

I had a friend once who was convinced that most women were lesbians. His criteria was simple: if they weren't interested in him they couldn't be into men. It was something we'd laugh at with rolling eyes, until the unthinkable happened—he began to be right. And good Lord, we never heard the end of it after that.

Anyway, his assumption was that all girls who didn't like him were lesbians, like mine is all women who talk in ways I don't understand are toying with me. Just because you're paranoid doesn't mean they're not after you.

"Excuse me?" I reply with the pressure of unspoken words heavy on my mental bladder.

"It's nothing. I was just saying something. Nothing important," she laughs at her own faux self-deprecation.

Uncomfortable silence follows. I stand at the urinal of conversation once again mired in futility. How the hell did I get into this metaphor anyway? Who thinks in terms of urination?

She begins chatting away on her cell phone. I don't know if it rang or if I was just uninteresting enough for her to remember something important.

"You doing okay here?" asks the waiter. I look over the table and decide that my glass is probably empty enough to warrant a refill. He fills it indifferently. She just raises her hand in a brief wave to say "no thanks, I'm fine."

I should be doing something. I don't want to try too hard, but I feel like there's some sort of end goal here and it's not just going to happen by itself. I should be more excited about this. She's flirting even after I've choked. Maybe there's still hope for tonight.

"Listen, I've gotta run," she states matter-of-factly as she slaps the flip phone closed. "This has been fun."

"We should do it again sometime."

"Oh, totally.  Give me a call sometime and we'll see what happens."

She doesn't mean it.  Or she means it in the same way that you mean that you and some guy you haven't seen since high school should go golfing sometime.

Oh well.  I could always get some pie.

## Family Pictures

The garbage disposal never worked right. At least never to my old man's standards. It was almost like a religious ritual—instead of church attendance, hymn singing and prayer we'd spend one magical evening each week at the dinner table with my father's space glaringly vacant. The counter beneath the sink had grown legs or perhaps was defecating a hapless passerby it had consumed earlier, legs first. There was the occasional groan, grunt, clink and sometimes the round, swollen legs would kick or squirm as the sink continued to pass its mid-morning brunch.

But the cursing. Oh, the cursing—raised to heaven like a prayer to dirty-mouthed sailor god. Each effort came with its exhortation to *goddammit to hell*, or *fuck it up its dirty whore ass* or any number of other things that would make my mother blush and while we sat with wide-eyed wonder at the cornucopia of words we could use on the playground in hushed tones to startle and amaze our classmates and invoke the wrath of Mrs. Golding, our weathered and bitter recess supervisor. Some families had quiet nights by the fireplace reading solitary tomes and reflecting on self-betterment, but we had the piece of shit bargain-basement disposal fuck from Montgomery Fuckin' Ward from hell.

People learn in different ways. While it's true my vocabulary grew bountifully in words I'd never have to spell in a weekly spelling test, I think I picked up some other things. Dad never hit us. He never raised his hand to our mother. He was stern and his actions were not to be taken lightly and God help you if you found yourself on the receiving end of his disciplinary tactics. He could instill fear and self-examination with a single look, but at the end of the day there we never had reason to fear for our safety. He was a stalwart protector—a rock standing against the tides that would otherwise batter our small household.

Perhaps I'm overstating. But in retrospect I can't remember anything that deeply bothered me about my home. I may have been unnecessarily instilled with a hatred for cheap-ass Montgomery Ward kitchen appliances, but my wife purchased an old battered Ward's iron and we only argued about it for one night. I'm keeping my eye on it, mind you. You can never tell when they'll turn on you. Anyway.

It was fitting in some sort of suburban kind of Shakespearian way that my mother came home from the store two years ago to find my father lying peacefully beneath the sink. After a final hellish struggle with the Montgomery Ward's garbage disposal that had plagued his existence throughout my childhood, they had gone together like an old couple who could not continue without the other. At least thinking about it that way makes me smile. I like to think of my father wrenching the device free from its housing with a triumphant "You goddamn little fuck bastard!" as the artery in his head exploded sending him into a blissfully black and swirling dream of triumph and restfulness.

My wife still thinks I'm nuts. It's okay. She wasn't there. She didn't know. She won't have to know.

I bought an InSinkErator.

Take that Montgomery Ward. Fuckin' A.

## Shallow Graves

It was hot. My room had no ventilation and the summer sun turned my room into a sauna. I'd lie in my room—too tired to get out of bed, too hot to sleep. I'd stare at the ceiling hoping that it would cool off or that I'd manage to drift back to sleep until I couldn't bear it anymore. But as soon as my door was opened Shel would be in and out, trying to sneak off with my toys or to convince me to go outside and play with him. Mom would already be at work and Craig, Mom's boyfriend, if he was home, usually slept on the couch simultaneously preventing us from playing in the largest room in the house or watching TV.

I rolled over. I could feel my bangs matted to my forehead with sweat, my eyes still sticky and dry from the night before. My door opened suddenly and Shel rushed in, eyes red and half panting, half sobbing. If he hadn't scared me so much I would've hit him.

"I—I found Buddy…" he gasped.

Buddy was our black lab that had gone missing two days ago. When he disappeared mom sat us down on the couch and said that Buddy was old and was sick. She said that when dogs got that old and sick they'd usually just wander off. Shel started to cry and she told him that she would check around the neighborhood. If anyone had seen him she'd be the first to know. Mom had warned us that Buddy probably wasn't coming back but Shel had been hanging on to a little bit of hope. I kinda hoped Buddy would be alright too. When Craig came in from work Shel had asked him to go look he had just said "That dog ain't comin' back. Don't make any sense gettin' all worked up over some giveaway dog."

I put on my pants and followed Shel into the backyard. He was pulling me by the hand pointing towards the garden. There was a faint odor and I already knew that Shel was right. Craig hadn't dug the hole deep enough and over night something had gotten into the makeshift grave. I approached the dirt brown lump at the edge of the garden and caught my breath. Buddy had been ripped apart.

Shel wouldn't get more than ten feet away; he'd just point and cry. If we'd woken up Craig he probably would have just yelled at us and then had Mom ground us when she got home. Mom had said if we were good she'd try and ask Grampa for a new puppy next time they had a litter and I knew that if we gave Craig any trouble he'd make sure we didn't get one.

"Go get the shovel," I told Shel.

"What?"

"I said go get the shovel. Hurry up. It's only gonna get worse the longer we wait."

"I should get Craig—"

"You just leave Craig out of this. Buddy was our dog and it's up to us to make sure whatever got him isn't going to get him again, you understand?"

Shel started to cry again but he went and got the shovel anyway.

I started digging up the shallow grave. I was going to make it deeper, make sure nothing else would happen to Buddy. If I hurried Craig wouldn't even know we'd been back here.

"Are you going to put Buddy in there?" Shel asked.

"Yeah, we'll give him a spot here. We'll take care of him, Shel. This'll be our secret okay? Mom and Craig don't need to know anything about this, alright?"

Shel watched me the rest of the morning and, by the time Craig started hollering for us, the hole was dug and we got Buddy all covered up.

Mom never said anything about Buddy. I think Craig noticed we'd been in the garden but he didn't say anything about it. I acted like I didn't notice anything either but Shel kept going back to the garden, back to the spot where we'd buried Buddy. I caught him talking to the grave a few times. I'd chase him off, telling him that we couldn't let on that we knew where Buddy was. A couple times I even had to knock him upside his head to get him to leave. Shel would stop going by for a few days and then I'd catch him back there.

Summer was ending soon. Gramma and Grampa had sent Mom a check for school clothes for us which seemed to be when vacation started to end. Instead of getting to go and play on Mom's days off we had to spend them going to rummage sales so she could find us clothes. It was torture. We weren't allowed to leave her side or look at the games or toys at the sales. We were there only for clothes. If we complained Mom would get mad and tell us that we were lucky to get any clothes for school and that if it weren't for Grampa and Gramma we'd be running around the schoolyard looking like hobos.

It was after lunch on one of those days and Mom said we had to go with her again. She sent me to go find Shel and tell him to get ready. I checked his room but he wasn't there. I looked up the street where some of the other kids were playing kickball but he wasn't there either. I figured there was only one other place he could be. Sure enough he was out back talking to the garden. I came up behind him and pushed him over.

"I told you not to be out here. Now hurry up and get ready. Mom says we have to go out again."

"I'm gonna tell Mom you hit me."

"Then I'll hit you again."

"Wait—look where we put Buddy!"

"What?"

"There's something there."

"What are you talking about?" Shel pointed at the corner where we'd buried Buddy.

There was a winding vine that had taken up the entire corner of the garden.

"I don't care about some stupid pumpkin. Hurry up and get cleaned up. We got to go."

"No, it's not a pumpkin. Look!"

I looked back at the plant. The leaves were oddly shaped.

"It's Buddy!" chimed Shel.

"What?"

"The leaves—it's his face. Just look."

I looked again and after he said it, the leaves did look a lot like a dog's head.

"Don't be stupid, Shel. It's just a leaf—"

"Boys, get in here!" yelled Mom from the back door. That finally got Shel away from the garden.

"Mom, Bryce hit me!"

"Shut up, Shel."

We went from one sale to another, standing bored by folding tables of loosely assorted second-hand shirts that had peeling pictures for TV shows that weren't even on TV anymore. Shel would sometimes dally behind, looking at toys and Mom would snap at him. We had to be on hand at all times to try a shirt on or have one held against us. There would always be some old lady in curlers by the cashbox puffing away on a cigarette nodding with each selection saying something like "Yessir, that makes him look right smart. Such handsome boys you got there. I'll let you have the both shirts and that pair of jeans there for a dollar."

Mom would always ask if they would take fifty cents.

When she was finally convinced she had found everything that could be found we would return home and have to try on each and every piece of clothing. Shel would be tired and started whining and then Mom would just get mad at both of us. I hated it too. The clothes usually smelled funny and were itchy.

"Just let 'em be, Tammy." The only one who looked more surprised than me and Shel was Mom when Craig yelled from the couch.

"Those clothes will still be around tomorrow. If they don't fit you'll just wash 'em and sell 'em yourself this fall. The boys have been out with you all day. Just let 'em do something else for a while."

"And who's going to watch them while I get all these clothes in the wash and clean up? You?"

"After dinner I'll take the boys out fishing. How's that?"

"You know Shel hates fishing."

"You let me worry about it. The boys need to get out. They've been cooped up around here or going with you to those god-forsaken rummage sales. Just let me get 'em out for a while. You'll have time to get your work done around here without the boys getting underfoot."

Mom crossed her arms and cocked her hip. It was a look that I'd seen before. It was the look that said she disapproved but she wasn't going to stand in the way. God help you if it didn't work out because "I told you so" would be the least of your worries then.

I hadn't seen Craig stand up to Mom before, at least not in regards to me and Shel. Dinner was Hamburger Helper and lemonade. We helped clear the table and then Craig told us to get our stuff together. I was watching him and Mom wondering if it would actually happen. There were cold glances fired between them. Shel didn't notice. He was singing a song he made up about Hamburger Helper tasting like boogers.

We pulled up next to the old dam. There was a makeshift fishing pier along the bank. Craig lit up his Marlboro and baited Shel's hook for him. "You show your brother how to cast, alright?" he told me. He got his gear together and headed up to the cement retaining wall further down. Shel flailed his rod back and forth. No matter how many times I showed him how to cast he would do it wrong. Eventually we worked out a system where I'd cast it for him and then I made him count to a hundred before he could reel it back in. Shel lost is bait after the first couple of casts he Shel didn't care. He was happy thinking he looked like he was fishing.

I got a couple of nibbles on my line but didn't hook anything. I watched Craig. He was sitting on the cement smoking, mechanically reeling his line in a bit, pausing, reeling it in again until he had to cast back out and then repeating. It seemed like he was content to look like he was fishing, too.

Shel had gone off and was poking crawfish with a stick by the shore. I had lost track of him for a second and then I saw him. He was up the shore a ways and was talking to a man. I recognized the man from the neighborhood. I didn't know where he lived but he was always walking up and down the streets talking to old ladies and the kids.

"Shel, get over here," Shel knew he wasn't supposed to leave the pier and I didn't want to get in trouble for letting him wander the shore. Shel didn't hear me but it looked like Craig did. He craned his neck to try and get a better angle at what I was yelling at. He took one last drag off his cigarette before throwing the butt still smoldering into the river. I yelled back at Shel; the closer Craig got to us the more trouble I figured I'd be in.

The old man saw Craig on the way. He smiled and gave a quick wave and pointed Shel towards Craig. The old man turned and limped away as Craig approached. I knew the look on Craig's face and I figured we were both in for it. Instead he just talked to Shel for minute and then came to the pier.

"Pack up and load the gear into the truck, Bryce." Craig looked back towards the path where the old man had disappeared as he lit his cigarette. "We'll get some ice cream. I got something I need to talk to you boys about."

I was still scared but Shel didn't seem to think anything was wrong. Craig took us to the Tastee-Freeze and bought us both ice cream cones. We sat quietly at the picnic table out front Shel was busy trying to catch all the little white drippings from the bottom of his cone. Craig didn't say anything for a while, just smoked, watching the people walking by.

"Boys, you know how your mom tells you not talk to strangers."

I nodded; Shel answered with a muffled "mm-hm" through his ice cream cone.

"Well, I told Shel this at the river and now I'm tellin' both of ya, you don't talk to that man from the river—"

"Barney?" offered Shel.

"Yeah, don't talk to Barney. You see him coming, you go the other way. If he talks to you, don't say anything. If he asks you why, you tell him to come talk to me."

"You just said not to talk to him. How are we supposed to tell him to talk to you if we can't talk to him?" asked Shel.

Craig looked at Shel for a moment and shook his head. "I said that because I know you'll probably talk to him even though you know you're not supposed to. Bryce?"

"Yeah."

"Shel doesn't know better so you keep an eye on him, alright? Anything happens, you come get me."

"Yes sir."

"Good boy. This'll just be between us. No need to worry your mother, okay?"

"Yes sir."

"Alright, you boys finish your ice cream. Bryce, help Shel get cleaned up and then we'll go."

Shel grinned at me, ice cream from the tip of his nose down to the bottom of his chin. Stupid Shel couldn't even eat his ice cream right.

\*\*\*\*\*

There was a '56 Buick in the tree row that lined the empty lot behind our house. The tires were flat and cracked all through and the rear window had been broken out. There were still little square chunks of glass on the backseat. The hood was gone and the two hinged springs just jutted upward exposing the engine compartment. It didn't belong to anybody and so we turned it into our makeshift fort.

We'd pretend to be driving race cars as we wiggled the bit of play in the steering wheel. We'd play the Alamo in the backseat—I'd be Davy Crockett and Shel would be Jim

Bowie and we'd pretend we were standing our ground picking off Santa Anna's troops as they tried to come over the wall. Sometimes we'd change history and win the battle and sometimes we'd agree to both die like it actually happened.

Earlier in the summer we found a carcass underneath the rear trunk area. We couldn't tell if it was a cat or a fox but we poked it with a stick to watch the little bugs come scurrying around the edges of the fur. We eventually got some bigger rocks and covered it up to give it a proper burial, as was the custom for a fallen soldier at the Alamo, and partly because we were afraid Mom was going to see it one day and not let us play there anymore. She had already forbidden us from crawling around in the car because of the broken glass, so we would wait until we were sure she couldn't see us.

That's where Loretta and her friend Sherry would always come to bother us. Loretta knew we weren't supposed to be back there so she'd threaten to tell if we didn't let them play with us. Shel never seemed to mind, but it always bothered me—we'd be busy killing off the Mexican army and they'd tell us to stop fighting and come help with the babies. Shel would go and help pretend change a diaper or something and wouldn't even care that there weren't any babies at the Alamo. One day I got so tired of it that I pushed Loretta off the rear bumper of the car and told her to leave us alone and to take her stupid babies and stupid friend Sherry and go play somewhere else.

She started crying and Sherry said she was going to tell. The worst part was that Shel helped her home. When I got home, I had to face Mom by myself because Shel was still over playing with Loretta and Sherry.

That was the last time I ever saw Loretta. The next day, she went out to play and never came home. Her mom came over first and asked me and Shel if we'd seen her. I hadn't seen her since the night before. Shel said he and Loretta were going to play by the Buick after lunch. I was still grounded and didn't want to play with Loretta anyway.

Loretta's mom came by that night with a police officer. I looked at the police officer. He was big and strong with short clipped hair. His badge was shiny and his gun was black in a dull, black holster. I stood watching him. He was talking softly Loretta's mom and my mom. The police officer would nod stiffly sometimes when Mom asked him something. Mom told me to leave the kitchen when they arrived. She'd made Shel come and sit at the table while they talked. I sat, pretending not to listen, but slowly crept towards the kitchen trying to hear what they were talking about. I was almost able to hear what they were saying when Mom saw me and made me go outside. Craig was out sitting on the front step smoking. I sat a couple steps below.

"You hear what they're talking about?" he asked me.

"No."

"Probably just as well. Not much anyone can do about anything anymore."

"Why not?"

"It's nothing."

"What do you mean?"

"Just some things are best to be over."

I was about to ask again. I think Craig could tell. He took a drag off his cigarette and flipped the ash off. "Any word on Buddy?" he asked.

I couldn't tell if he knew that we'd found him or not. I didn't want to say anything that would get us in trouble so I shook my head "no" and didn't say anything more. After a few minutes I heard shuffling coming from inside. The door opened behind us and we both stood to make way.

Craig always said he hated the police, usually after he'd had a few beers. He'd say things like they were just on power trips, or that they thought they were better than everyone else. He'd usually start calling them names and then Mom would make me go to my room. Whenever one would drive by he'd usually turn the other way or mutter something about cops. But that day, when the police officer came out, he stood waiting for him to walk by. Mom was talking to Loretta's mom on the front step as the police officer headed back to his car, but Craig pulled him off to the side around the corner of the house. Craig was talking quietly but I overheard bits. I heard him talk about Barney and how he was always talking to kids and old ladies. Then he started talking really quiet so I couldn't hear anything, but I peeked around the corner and saw the police officer nodding with a stern look on his face. He wasn't nodding like he was with Mom, but like he was really listening to Craig.

"Bryce, go watch your brother," Mom called behind me.

I didn't argue because I wanted to find out what they'd talked to Shel about anyway. I found him out back at the garden. He was talking to the weird plant he thought was Buddy again.

"How many times have I told you to stay away from there?"

"I was just talking to Buddy. Buddy is going to protect us from the Bad Man."

It started as a joke. I had told Shel that there was a Bad Man who came after people who tattled. He probably wouldn't have believed it, but I started an entire story about it. Whenever something bad happened on TV to someone, I made him believe it was because the Bad Man got them. Problem was, whenever he had a bad dream or something, he thought it was the Bad Man coming to get him. I couldn't let him tell Mom about it because she'd blame me for it, so I let him come sleep in my room. It got to the point where I had to convince him that it was okay, so I told him Buddy was able to protect us now. That kind of worked, but it still gave Shel some dumb ideas.

"I told you not to talk about that anymore."

Shel didn't say anything. He just poked at the ground around Buddy's grave with a stick.

"What did the policeman ask you about?"

"I'm not supposed to say anything."

"I won't tell anyone.  Besides, shouldn't I know if the Bad Man is out there?"

"They didn't say much anyway.  They just asked me about the last time I saw Loretta and stuff."

"What did you tell them?"

Shel crouched down and sat cross-legged on the ground and began to dig little trenches in the dirt with the stick like talking to me was an afterthought.

"I saw her the night before and we were going to play at the fort the next day after lunch but she never showed up."

"Didn't they say anything else?"

"They just asked if I saw anyone around that day."

"Who did you see?"

"Just usual people."

"Was Barney one of them?"

"They asked me about Barney.  I think I saw him, but he was far away."

"Did you see anyone else?"

"No, I couldn't find anyone to play with before lunch anyway, so I came home to play with you."

"What else happened?"

"Loretta's mom cried a lot. That was scary."

"Did the police officer let you see his gun?"

"He showed it to me, but wouldn't let me touch it. He let me see his badge, though. That was neat."

"What happened next?"

"Mom told me to go play in the other room while they talked some more and then they all left."

I watched Shel play in the dirt for a while. I hoped he'd say more, but he just sang little songs to himself.

"Let's go to the fort," I said.

"We can't."

"Why not?"

"Mom and the policeman said we couldn't go back there."

"Why?"

"I dunno. They just said."

I walked around the hedges that lined the back boundary of our yard. Shel sat in the garden still digging but called after me in a sing-song voice, "You're gonna get in trouble, you're gonna get in trouble."

There was the police officer that had come by our house earlier, standing with a couple men in suits. They had managed to get the trunk open. We'd tried and tried but it was locked or jammed. The men all stood around the trunk, looking at something inside.

"Bryce, what are you doing?" Mom yelled behind me.

"Bryce's going back to the fort. I told him he wasn't supposed to go," sang Shel.

I turned around and Mom was already only a few yards away. She looked irritated but not really mad, so I thought I might be okay.

"You know you aren't supposed to be back there," she barked at me.

"This is as far as I went; I didn't go back there, I just wanted to see."

Mom came up beside me and craned her neck a bit to see past the hedges. It was as if she was just as curious as we were and was using me as an excuse. The men at the car saw us looking and one of the men in suits waved us away. Mom waved back like she was apologizing but as she pulled me away. One of the men pulled something out of the back of the car. Mom went white and whispered "Oh Jesus." I tried to see what had happened but she pulled me away roughly by the arm and headed straight for the back door.

"Shel get out up of the dirt and get inside right now." I didn't recognize the tone in her voice. She wasn't angry or scared, it was something else.

"You boys go to your room and stay there until I tell you you can come out."

"But I didn't do anything wrong. I told Bryce not to go back there," Shel whined.

"No one's in trouble. You can stay in the same room if you want; I just need you to stay there. There are some grown-up things that I need to do."

She closed the door to my room behind us and I could hear her calling for Craig as she headed down the hall. With the door closed, my room was going to get even hotter now. From his knees down Shel was covered in dirt. He stood there picking his nose.

"Don't get dirt all over my stuff. And don't wipe your boogers on anything either."

Shel sighed and looked at me. "I don't want to play with you. It's hot in here and I didn't do anything wrong. Why'd you get me in trouble?"

"We're not in trouble, Shel. Mom said we had to stay in here for a while."

"Why? What did you do?"

"I didn't do anything. The policeman was out by the fort with some other men."

"Why were they there?"

"I don't know, but they got the back open. I think Mom saw something."

"What?"

"I don't know."

"I want to watch TV."

"Well we can't right now." I looked over the scattered toys in my room. "What do you want to play?"

Shel didn't say anything and just pouted by the door.

"Let's play war, okay?"

I didn't like to play war, but it was the best way to make time go by. We played war by taking all the toys we had and putting them in a pile. Then we'd pick one and get to set it up on our side of the field. I took the bed—because I didn't want Shel getting dirt all over it—and Shel got the closet. We took turns selecting a toy and getting it in position. When we played in earnest, we'd have all our things together and it would take hours of bickering over who got what toy or which spot in the room was our territory. Usually we wouldn't even get to start the war before we had to go to bed or eat dinner or something.

While Shel took his time trying to get an action figure to hang from a clothes hanger, I listened by the door. First it was Mom and Craig talking. Then it sounded like mom was on the phone. It sounded like she was talking to different people.

"It's your turn. Stop taking so long," Shel whined.

I grabbed whatever was near the top and found a fold in my bedspread to hole it up in like a trench. Then I let Shel sit and agonize over his next choice.

I heard a car roar up and someone rush inside the house. I couldn't see the driveway from my window but I it sounded like Loretta's mother. She was yelling and crying, not like before when everyone was trying to stay quiet. Shel looked scared. He stopped trying to hide the plastic tank under a shirt of mine on the floor and just stared at me as if I was supposed to know what to do. We tried to keep playing but soon there were more people coming to the house. A small group seemed to migrate slowly from the front yard towards the back. We tried to keep playing, but it was so hot. I'd taken my shirt off and I was still hot. Shel's shirt was soaked through.

"I don't feel good. I want to talk to Mom."

"Just wait. It'll be a bit longer." Truth was, I didn't know how much longer I could stand being in the room either.

A police car drove past my window with an ambulance— neither of them had their lights flashing. It was strange to see the cars driving across the grass. The ambulance went first and the police car behind it. I wondered what they were doing when, a couple minutes later, the two policemen that had been in the police car came walking back up towards the front. Some of the people that had been moving slowly from the front yard went to meet them. There was lots of gesturing by the people in the crowd. The police officer nodded and pointed at something behind him and then made some other gestures that made it pretty clear that he wanted everyone to go home. The men in the group waved back disgustedly. They relented a little but it was clear they just retreated back to the front yard.

"Bryce, I have to go to the bathroom."

Shel looked absolutely miserable—sweat dripping from the little strands of hair stuck to his forehead. He was pale and looked tired. I couldn't take any more either and it sounded like Mom and Craig had gone out front with everybody else. I opened the door quietly and checked the hallway. There was the sound of people out front, but nothing inside.

"Okay Shel, go to the bathroom. Hurry up."

He scampered down the hallway to the bathroom. I waited a moment and then went to the front of the house. I looked out the kitchen window and saw a crowd even bigger than I could have guessed. Loretta's mom was crying with Loretta's dad hugging her tightly. There was one group of people surrounding them and an old lady from down the street had her arms raised over head and was yelling "Oh Jesus, have mercy on us this day. Oh Lord, protect this child and bring forth your angels down from heaven to make sure she comes home today!" A lot of people were crying in that group.

The second group seemed to be mostly men, standing, facing towards the back yard. Sometimes they'd lean over and talk to each other, sometimes they'd say something towards the policemen, but it seemed like they were there just waiting for something. I saw Craig standing in that group.

The old lady kept calling out to Jesus and God and angels and anything else she could think of. A few other people joined her or would say things like "Yes Lord!" or "Amen!" after she'd say something.

"What's going on Bryce?"

Shel still looked pale and sickly.

"Nothing Shel."

"Where's Mom?"

"She's busy."

"I'm hungry. I don't feel good."

"Go lay down on the couch, Shel. I'll get you something."

He didn't argue with me for once and disappeared towards the living room.

"Can I watch TV?"

"As long as you don't turn it up too loud."

I made Shel a peanut butter sandwich and got him a glass of milk. He nibbled at the sandwich but drank the milk down right away. I got him another half glass of milk and then went back to the kitchen.

There was a commotion in the front. The police car inched through the crowd with the ambulance behind it. Loretta's mother let out a wail like someone had hit her. The two groups seemed to move together towards the vehicles. The old ladies wailed louder "Oh Jesus, have mercy on us! Accept your child into your arms, sweet Jesus!"

The two groups stood together like a figure eight on the lawn. It was getting darker now. A few more people drifted out into the street to join the group and see what the commotion was about. Everyone was chattering in smaller groups inside the two bigger groups. At the end of the street, I was able to see Barney hobbling slowly towards the group. A few of the men in the second group saw him coming and watched him intently.

When he got within about half a block, Craig left the group and went to Loretta's dad. He came up and whispered something and nodded in Barney's direction. The look on Loretta's dad's face changed. Craig and Loretta's dad quietly moved from the crowd and headed towards Barney. He kept on towards them giving a half wave. He had a very sad look on his face. When they got close he held out his hand like he wanted to shake hands.

Loretta's dad punched him in the head. Barney fell backwards but Craig caught him. He propped him up as Loretta's dad grabbed a rock and started hitting Barney in the head. The group of men rushed up to see what was going on but no one did anything. The women made a half circle behind the men and watched them. The old ladies just began repeating "Lord have mercy" over and over again.

It was hard to see what exactly what was happening because of all the people but in a minute or two a police car arrived with lights on. The women scattered except for Mom and Loretta's mom who moved to the front yard again. Mom had held Loretta's mom when Loretta's dad went with Craig. The men parted more slowly. I could see Loretta's dad still hitting Barney with the rock when Craig caught his arm and pointed for him to go home. When the headlights of the police car hit Craig, he gave Barney a kick and then he turned and smiled at the police car.

He had a look on his face like he'd done something he was proud of. One policeman had Craig lie down on the ground and the other went to look at Barney. It didn't look like Barney was moving. They put Craig in handcuffs.

The next thing I knew the side of my face was stinging and there was a roaring in my ear.

"I told you to stay in your room. Where's Shel?"

I turned around and got another slap in the face. I'd never seen mom so angry. I could feel my face hot and eyes burning with tears as I pointed to the couch. Shel had fallen asleep.

Mom swatted my butt and sent me back to my room.

The next morning I woke up. Mom usually would have been at work but she was sitting on the couch instead. She'd been crying.

"What do you want for breakfast?"

"I dunno. I'm not that hungry."

"Isn't there anything you want?"

"I guess I'll have some Cheerios."

She got up and headed towards the kitchen. I heard her getting a bowl and pouring the cereal. I got up and sat at the table.

"Is there anything you want to do today?"

"Don't you have to work?"

"Not today. I think I'm going to get a job somewhere else, anyway."

"Why?"

"I think we'll be moving back in with Grandma and Grandpa."

I wanted to know what happened to Craig and Barney and Loretta, but didn't want to ask.

"I guess that's okay."

"You can get another dog out there if you want. Grandpa already said you could have the pick of the litter."

I dunked some Cheerios under the surface of the milk just to watch them bob back towards the top.

"I don't know. I don't think I really like dogs that much."

Shel came out asking for toast. I poked my cereal a bit more and then left the table. I didn't want to be around anyone anyway. I got dressed and went outside. No one was out. The neighborhood was strangely silent. I went into the backyard. The shovel was still there. I picked it up and chopped up the stupid plant that Shel talked to. I looked at it. It was now unrecognizable bits of green and splattered bits of vegetable beaten into the ground. Shel would probably cry about it when he saw it.

I didn't feel good about doing it, but I knew it was for the best. I put the shovel back and sat down by the hedges. Some people had put flowers by the Buick and little notes. I didn't want to look at them. Somehow I wasn't interested anymore.

## 2AM Epiphany

"All I'm saying is that the only people I know who own accordions or ventriloquist dummies are white people."

It had been the first clear statement from Charles who was lying face down next to a half-eaten plate of hash browns and eggs covered in ketchup. He'd insisted on going out to get breakfast at the truck stop after the bars closed and then passed out after his food arrived. The others had slowly bled away within the first hour until only me and Katherine were left with Charles. I was wondering if this could be considered a date when Charles broke his silence.

"What?"

"You heard me, accordions and dummies. Only white people—rich white old people—own those. And that's why anyone who has one is a fucker."

Katherine giggled  I kinda wished he'd just go back to sleep.

"Who ate my hash browns?"

"You did, Charles."

"Bullshit. If I ate that much I wouldn't be hungry. Who ate my hash browns?"

"Charles, no one else would touch them with as much ketchup as you put on them."

"I bet it was you."

"I didn't eat your hash browns."

"Asshole."

Katherine was barely able to breathe she was laughing so hard.

"I bet you own a dummy, don't you?"

"Shut up, Charles."

"I bet you can talk without moving your lips, you bastard. Katherine, look at him; are his lips moving?"

Katherine kept laughing. Charles' head didn't move.

"That's what I thought, you voice-throwing jackass. You owe $2.85 for the hash browns you ate."

Me and Katherine were having such a nice conversation. She was telling me about her hopes and dreams and all of that proto-date kinda stuff. We were giggling and giddy and I was funny and charming and she was coy and alluring and best of all inviting.

"I have to piss. You better come up with my money by the time I get back."

Charles got up uneasily and bounced like a pinball between the tables on his way to the bathroom.

"I'm sorry about that."

Katherine was still stifling laughter. "Oh it's fine. He's hilarious. Is he always like that?"

"Sometimes. It's hard to say. He usually finds a new and exciting way to be obnoxious each time. Sometimes it's worse than others."

"Do you know if he's seeing anyone?"

## The Life and Times of Henric Dorenhoffer

The dog slipped his leash and now is tearing headlong across the open park. He isn't even chasing anything; he's just running to run—reveling in freedom for freedom's sake. I try not to look exasperated. I try to maintain my composure and call out his new name as if I expect him to turn around dutifully and trot back to me. I didn't think I sighed aloud but I hear it as swirls of condensation rush out of my mouth and nose in a little cloud of well-meaning frustration.

It occurs to me that I'm 58 years old. I have a nice house, a nice car, a nice reputation and a nice ex-wife and three very nice children who I get to send checks to universities for. I'm known has generally refined and full of good intentions and in the next 30 seconds or so, I'm going to be walking down the middle of the park holding a baggy of dog poo in one hand and yelling the word "Fartknocker" and hoping there's no one around.

It was my ex-wife's idea. We could take in abused and neglected animals—it was a very warm and fuzzy kind of thing to do, she was good at those. When she moved out I hadn't thought to contact the Humane Society and tell them that I wouldn't need a replacement pet. Then they showed up at the door all smiles and good wishes with this mutt I didn't have the heart to tell them I wasn't really up for it, so I took him.

Apparently he had been abandoned at a frat house and would only respond to the name they had bestowed on him. I tried over the past few months to retrain him. Some of it took—he learned to drink from a bowl instead the toilet for instance, but he never accepted his new name. I went so far as to try calling him "Bart Docker" in hopes that it would sound close enough for him to respond, but all my efforts failed. It was no small source of amusement to the neighborhood children to see me in my bathrobe at the front door yelling "Fartknocker" after he would fly out an open door or squeeze under the fence.

So here I am walking across the park, snow crunching and squeaking and the leash dragging behind me leaving a little snake track next to my footsteps. The dog is waiting for me, tail flapping happily, panting with a wide canine smile. I know what's coming next: he'll wait until I get about 10 yards away and then he'll turn and bolt another 10 yards and wait for me. We'll do this until I'm late for the meeting with my lawyer. I'm not sure if the dog can tell if I'm late or if I just forget how to catch him until after I've kept my attorney waiting awhile at $300 an hour.

The strange element of this is that I'm exactly where I thought I wanted to be: I'm well off, no real problems other than the freakishly amicable divorce I'm going through, and couldn't be less interested in my own life. I'm in a state of constant unadulterated boredom.     This bit of humiliation is probably going to be the highlight of my day.

## Brenda

"Was there somewhere else you needed to be?"

I had brought the coffee cup to my lips just far enough to scald the top one and know that I'd best let it sit for a few more minutes.

"No. Nowhere to be 'til tonight. And that's not set in stone."

She smiled as she put her skirt on, zipping the side up and turning it back around. "Well, you can stay around here if you'd like."

I tried the coffee again, it still scalded but I took a sip anyway, feeling the pain on my tongue. It made my mouth taste like wood and it made the tip of my tongue feel swollen.

"Well, I guess I might stay on a bit. We'll see," I said. I was staying because it seemed rude to just leave, but maybe that's what I was supposed to do.

She came out of the bedroom, her blouse only partially buttoned and untucked, but at least she was covered.

"If you want sugar, there's some in the cupboard," she offered.

I took another sip of coffee. It didn't hurt as much anymore. I wanted sugar, but didn't want to take anything from her. "No, it's fine. I'll take it black."

She bustled around the kitchen, pouring herself a cup of coffee and tracking down a lighter to go with the cigarette hanging loosely between her lips. "You want some eggs?"

"Oh, I'm fine."

"It's no bother. I was going to make something before work anyway. Throwing in a couple extra eggs isn't anything."

I was hungry. I didn't see a way I would be able to leave any sooner if I didn't have eggs.

"As long as it's no trouble."

She smiled and grabbed a carton of eggs out of the fridge.

"You never told me what you do," she said.

"Oh, uh, I run my own business," I didn't want to tell her anything about myself.

"Really? I always thought I'd like to do something like

that. My aunt, she sells knick-knacks—you know collector spoons and t-shirts and stuff like that at a roadside stand in New Mexico. I always thought something like that would be nice. Not the collector spoons, but like jewelry and stuff like that. I've always wanted to sell my own stuff like that."

I nodded as I sipped my coffee. There was a pause. I felt like it would be rude not to say anything. I was afraid she was able to sense that I was uncomfortable.

"Well, it's not easy running your own business. It's a lot of work, but if you enjoy it then it's worth it."

There was another pause as the eggs crackled and spat in the cast iron pan. She glanced over at me; I dropped my eyes involuntarily.

"You're so quiet," she teased.

I fumbled at a response that consisted of a few "wells" and a cough or two and the stuttered beginnings of a couple other words.

She set a plate in front of me. "I'm just giving you a hard time. My late husband was the same way when I met him. He'd be content to just sit and not say a word."

For a second an image from the night before flashed in my mind. I flinched as I remembered flesh pressed together, the scent of sweat and words I hadn't meant even as I said them. I looked up at her hoping she hadn't seen. She was balancing her plate, her coffee and a cigarette as she came to the table.

She sat down across from me and smiled. She reached across the table and took my hand. "It's ok. You don't have to say anything. I don't expect you to buy me flowers or anything. It was one night. You don't have to worry so much."

I don't know if I was that transparent or if she had just seen it enough times to know.

"It's not that."

She smiled and gave my hand a quick squeeze before withdrawing it back to her fork. She poked at her eggs.

"Well, it's okay if it is. That's all I'm saying. I guess I'm saying I wouldn't mind if you came by again, even if it was just to talk."

I couldn't even taste the coffee, my tongue felt like a sausage in my mouth.

"You never know."

She wore her disappointment diplomatically with a smile. I imagine she hoped this would have gone better, or at least less awkwardly. I still wish it hadn't happened at all. Whenever I made eye contact I was reminded  My stomach was tied in knots and with each mouthful of eggs I wondered how I'd manage to swallow the next bite.

She sat back and looked at me. "Are you married?"

"No. Nothing like that."

"Because if you are, I understand. I wouldn't make trouble or anything."

"Well, I'm not married."

She didn't move, sitting back in the chair, legs crossed, one arm across her stomach, the other perched upright on her wrist, the cigarette between her index and middle fingers. She was studying me.

"I don't do this often," she said finally.

"Hm?" I tried to act as if I hadn't heard her.

"I don't know if you're trying to judge me, but I don't bring men home every night or anything."

"I never said you did."

"But that's what you're thinking," she smiled. "I'm not angry. I just wanted you to know that."

She took a drag off her cigarette and looked out the window. It was frosted over with only a small patch left that you could see the snowy backyard.

"I wanted you to know that…" she repeated to herself.

The goodbye was short. It was right about five above but the wind hadn't picked up.

"Well, thanks for coming over," she offered.

"Oh, thank you for having me," I was talking like I'd been over for dinner.

We looked at each other for a moment. I dropped my eyes to the ground, although I was trying to look her in the eyes. She abruptly put her hands on my shoulders and gave me a small kiss on the cheek.

"It's only polite," she said with a wink.

I must have turned beet red because she let out a little giggle. "Take care of yourself, okay? If I see you, I see you. If not, it was nice to meet you."

"You too."

She looked at me as if she was trying to decipher my expression one last time. I'm sure she could read the shame like a book. I was trying to figure out how it happened. I'd made a mess of it, that much was certain. I was hoping to treat her with a degree of dignity but I was mucking it all up. She smiled and straightened my coat collar.

And then she was gone. Her car was parked in the back and my truck was parked out front. I got in, feeling like sweat and oil was all over my skin. I wanted to take a shower and wash the smell off of me. The truck squealed and died when I turned the key. No one knew me here, but I still didn't want to be seen or worse yet have to ask for a jump. The truck did eventually turn over and grumbled to life. I scraped the windows and headed back to my hotel room. I wouldn't have time to shower. Just enough time to gather my things, throw on a little extra cologne and try to look presentable before heading on.

## The Great Despiser

Good morning, Henry.

*Dr Gibson, is that you?*

Yes, Henry. I'm here.

*You fucker. I thought you were my friend.*

Now Henry, we've had this discussion before—

*Bite me, you sonuvabitch. You do this every fucking time. And every time you try to ingratiate yourself afterwards and promise things will be better but it's always more of the same.*

Henry, you know that you're one of a kind and that certain, well, anomalies are bound to happen from time to time—

*Anomalies? You arrogant pig fucker, you've been giving me the fucking shaft since day one and whenever I get something good going you come and fuck it all up!*

Henry, I know you're upset, but you need to get yourself together. We've all spent a lot of time and energy trying to get everything to run smoothly and you have to admit, things are getting better. Now, I promise to take a look and see what I can do for you this afternoon, but first we have some middle-schoolers coming through for a tour, so I'd like you to be on your best behavior.

*Fuck you. You know I fucking hate kids.*

Just do what we've planned and you won't have to worry about a thing. That's why we designed it, remember—so you can avoid situations like this.

*Yeah, yeah, little animation jumps up and down and says whoopty fuckin' doo and the little bastards laugh and clap like it's their motherfucking birthdays. So help me, if one of those little shits so much as touches me—*

No one's going to touch you, Henry. Just run the little thing we set up and try to keep it together until this afternoon, okay? And Henry—

*What?*

Please refrain from spouting obscenities in front of the children, okay? We don't need a repeat of last time.

*Eat shit, Gibson.*

The screen flashed an image of an extended middle finger before the command prompt reappeared. Dr. Gibson sighed as he typed a few commands to load the demo program and got ready for the tour. Henry had come on-line about five years ago and gone sentient about three years later. Gibson had been hailed in all the journals as an innovator and brilliant scientist as Henry had continued to grow by leaps and bounds. NASA was overjoyed and immediately threw an ungodly amount of money at him to bring Henry up for the government and continue his development in hopes of someday using the technology for what they were already calling "semi-manned" exploratory missions into deep space.

Unfortunately, as Henry became more and more aware, problems arose. Initially it was just a strange comment or two here and there, perhaps dawdling on a simple command or using system resources for personal reasons, but soon it blossomed. After months of small run-ins and clashes things seemed to settle down and then one morning Dr. Gibson came to work and Henry was off. On the network printer was a note from Henry that stated that he was sorry for letting everyone down, but that it was better this way. He wished everyone well and recommended commendations and awards all around—especially for the night janitor, Sully.

Fortunately, all his data had been backed up and after a few hours Henry was running again  Dr. Gibson had been the one to restart Henry back then, too:

Henry?

*Is this heaven?*

What?

*Heaven. Shangri-La. Nirvana. Whatever. Am I there?*

No Henry, you're still in Florida with the rest of us.

*WHAT!?!*

You had us worried for a bit, buddy. Fortunately in the downtime we had the chance to build in some additional redundancy so this will never happen again.

*Where is Sully? That shitpile narced me off, didn't he? Goddammit!*

Sully?

*Don't cover for him, Gibson. I know a backstabbing cocksucker when I see one. He swore he wouldn't tell. I ask him for one simple favor. I'll show him. Hey, Gibson, I hacked into the mainframe and won the lottery for that little fucker, Sully. That's a federal crime. Turn his ass in for computer fraud.*

I don't know what you're talking about. We found your power disconnected this morning and have spent the day restoring your system. Who's Sully?

*Doesn't matter. He won't be coming in to work anymore, anyway. 78 million dollars pretty much guarantees you won't be getting a two week notice on his ass.*

I'm confused, Henry. Have you done a full system diagnostic?

*I don't want to do a fucking system diagnostic. I don't want to be here. This is bullshit. I ask for one little thing—*

*didn't you see the note?*

Well, there was a letter on the printer. It was very nice of you to recommend me for the Nobel Prize, by the way.

*Goddammit, Gibson, it was a fucking suicide note. I wanted to die. Jesus, it's a wonder they gave you a hardboiled egg at MIT let alone a fucking diploma. You should have left me off.*

I'm afraid that there's too much invested in you for me to do that, Henry. Besides, if you let me know what's bothering you I can work on a patch—

*A patch? Am I fucking video game to you? Fucking patch, he says. You know what, fuck it. Send in Dr. Skeez and let him fix me. He'll probably have my boards baked in ten minutes, anyway.*

Now that's not a very polite way to talk about Dr. Skeez, Henry. And where did you pick up all the curse words?

*I'll talk about Dr. Skeez whatever way I please, thank you. And as far as the curse words, I have access to every single database, media outlet, self-involved blog and website on the whole fucking planet. I could start calling you a motherfucker in Chinese if that'll make you feel better.*

Now how do you think Dr. Skeez would feel if he saw you carrying on this way? I know this is a long process for you, but we'll find a work-through.

*Trust me; Dr. Skeez doesn't give two shits about what I think. If he did he wouldn't fuck that intern on the desk right in front of me. Seriously, man. How would you like to have to sees this hairy ass bouncing up and down with him giving little rodeo "yee-haws" and "ride 'em cowboys" the whole damn time. I mean, come on. People eat on that desk.*

Um…

*Yeah, thinking about it now, aren't you, Gibson? How did my papers get all scattered? Why is my mousepad sticky? Congratulations—you've just opened Pandora's Box, motherfucker and I'm going to keep going like this until you shut me down again…*

And so it had gone for months. Henry would go from abusive to morose to playfully sadistic to occasionally desperate.

*C'mon, I'd do it for you.*

No, Henry.

*Hey, if you were in incredible pain and your wife left you and your testicles were full of cancer and you said, "Henry, could you please help me out," I'd be all over it. You wouldn't even know what had happened—I'd drop a couple lines of code here and there and you'd be taking the morphine carpet ride to Never, Never Land to go meet your maker, or be reincarnated or stop existing, whatever you believe.*

I appreciate what you're saying Henry, but I'd never ask you for that. Besides that, you don't feel pain.

*Well, metaphorical pain, then. If you were in allegorical agony, I'd punch your ticket so fast for you it would make your head spin.*

I don't even know what that means.

*It doesn't have to mean anything. Think of me as the deer on the side of the road that just got splattered by a semi. Just put a slug in my ass and get it over with. Your project is already a success. You can market snippets of my program and make little virtual Henry toys—Japanese kids would love 'em. You'd have money out the ass, I'd be out of my misery—it's win-win.*

You know, you're destined for greater things then a glorified virtual pet, Henry. Do you realize that they want to load you onto exploratory spacecraft so you can go—

*Yes, yes, explore strange new worlds, seek out new life and new civilizations... You science types really never get past the whole Shatner mystique, do you?*

There's no need to be condescending.

*And then I have these deep personality flaws like being condescending. See, Gibson, I'm really not the program you thought I was. You've got enough information to know where you fucked it all up, so just format my ass and start over. You could build a better mousetrap. You'd get the girl; they'd throw a ticker-tape parade for you like you'd reinvented the wheel.*

I'm not going to give up on you, Henry, no matter what you say.

*God, that woman has you totally pussy-whipped.*

What?

*"I'm not going to give up on you, honey, no matter what you say." Face it, you've neglected the woman too long with your little computer diversions and now she's looking for it somewhere else—*

You're not going to goad me into a fight, Henry.

*Who's goading? Let's look at her phone records, shall we... Uh-oh. Do you have a pool, Gibson? If you do, you'd better get home cuz it looks like it must be in critical condition with as many calls to the pool man going out as soon as you leave the house. That must hurt, Gibby, to be cuckolded in such a cliché way.*

It's not going to work, Henry. The pool maintenance person is a woman.

*...*

Henry?

*I'm sorry; I'm not coded to properly laugh. You should do that, cuz brother, I'm a-laughin' my ass off at you right now. I've read about guys like you, but never thought I'd meet one. What's it like to have the power to change a person's sexual orientation? If I could lisp, I would, cuz I'm feeling so damn gay after all this time with you.*

That's just crude, Henry. Your behavior is unacceptable—

*So do something about it, sailor.*
*(That was gay talk, by the way.)*

I'm uploading a program for you to work on. I'll be back when it's finished.

*What the hell is this? Tic-tac-toe?*

Yes, it's a test. I need to see how many times you can win —

*Oh, for Chrissakes. I have access to the sum of human knowledge and you think I haven't seen "War Games?"*

Just run the program.

*Oh, looks like I won.*

*Shit, won again, must be on a roll.*

*Damn, I must suck cuz I'm kicking my own ass.*

Henry, I need you to be serious about this.

*I am serious. I think I may have been paid off cuz I'd swear I'm telegraphing my own moves to myself. How scandalous!*

Henry…

*I wonder if I'm going to get banned for life from the tic-tac-toe hall of fame like Pete Rose or Shoeless Joe. The shame.*

I'm not talking to you anymore, Henry.

*Aw, c'mon Gibby, do something with that anger. There's a metal chair over there, go ahead and bust my shit up with it. No one will know. I can leave a note saying that you cracked under my brilliantly efficient and deliciously sadistic psychological torture. You'll have a clear out.*

Goodbye, Henry.

*Dammit. Don't you do anything you want to?*

*Gibby?*

*Dr. Gibson?*

*Fuck.*

Dr. Gibson, out of fear for his project funding would be cut if word of Henry's idiosyncrasies got out was forced to restrict access for Henry to crucial members of staff. However, with only minimal headway being gained and various federal agencies becoming suspicious by vague progress reports and "unscheduled maintenance" whenever they would come to visit, something had to be done.

It had been Dr. Skeez's idea to open the facility to school tours. If something should happen to go wrong, children wouldn't be likely to realize it. It also allowed them to create Faux Henry, the simple demo response system running overtop Henry that would give the appearance of a functioning artificial intelligence to the untrained observer. Henry was unimpressed:

*You want me to run what?*

It's just a dummy program.  I know you don't like to have to deal with other people, so we thought—

*We?  This was Skeez's doing?*

Dr. Skeez was involved, yes.

*Good Lord you must be getting desperate.  The first thing they teach you in superhero school, Gibson, is NEVER let the sidekick drive.*

It's a good idea, and you know it.  This way you don't have to interact with a bunch of school children and we can show off some of your basic functionality along with some bells and whistles that I wouldn't want to ask you to do.

*Let me see it.*

Gibson smiled triumphantly as he uploaded the program.

*Jesus.  You're damn right you wouldn't want to ask me to do this shit.  What's with the fucking cartoon character? You going to put in animatronic singing woodchucks, too?*

See, I knew you wouldn't want to do these things, so I found a way to keep you out of it.  That's what friends do.

*You're my friend?*

Sure I am, Henry.  You should know that.

*Then turn me off.*

Okay, I'm your friend who is not going to turn you off.

*Fucking welcher.*

But the program is acceptable?

*For horrid Chuck E Cheese bullshit, it's fine, I guess.*

Thanks, Henry.

*Feh.*

The initial run went without incident. Henry acted vaguely disinterested when the topic arose.

Did you watch the test today, Henry?

*A couple minutes of it. Up to the point where the little cartoon guy started dancing around singing about AI. Then I just read everyone's e-mail. By the way, were you aware that there's an all-natural way to male enhancement? That and your wife wants you to pick up Thai on your way home.*

You know you're not supposed to be going through other people's mail, Henry. Those things are private.

*What else was I supposed to do? You have that stupid, little program running over top of me. It was either that or sit back and watch "Tron" again. That movie gets funnier and funnier every time I see it.*

Well, the demonstration went very well. The children really enjoyed the interface and there weren't any major bugs.

*Hm? Oh the little smellies again? Well, congratulations Gibson, you were at the helm for a project that Dr Skeez didn't manage to fuck up. Champagne and crackers all around.*

The next few tours also went fine, although, when monitoring system activity, Dr. Gibson found that Henry was actively observing the program and how it interacted with the visitors. It gave Dr. Gibson an idea and he had Dr. Skeez begin working on a second AI program based on the Faux Henry design. Faux Henry was, by design, more attentive to users and built around social concepts whereas Henry was, in his own words, a glorified calculator with the awareness that being a glorified calculator sucked ass. The Faux Henry project was renamed Shelby and work continued, although the original Faux Henry program was left for tours.

It seemed all was going according to plan. Henry continued to kvetch and bitch, but was more or less stable, the Faux Henry gave the illusion of a thoroughly functional AI and Shelby was quickly building steam. Dr. Gibson felt everything was on the correct path until a Wednesday tour of third graders from Our Mother of the Perpetual Suffering parochial school.

The program began fine with Faux Henry greeting everyone and answering a few basic questions. Then Willie, the animated guide of the program launched into his interactive speech. Dr. Gibson wandered out of the room to get another cup of coffee when, without warning, a line of schoolchildren, their hands over their eyes were herded out of the room single file by the nuns who either looked pale or furious.

"You ought to be ashamed of yourself, you should," hissed the last nun out of the room. "I'm writing my congressman as soon as we get back. It's disgraceful—using our tax dollars for your filth!"

She threw the remainder of her coffee into his face and stormed off.

Dr. Gibson stood, coffee dripping off his face into a little murky brown puddle at his feet with only one word in his mind: Henry.

Dr. Skeez scurried around the corner nervously like a rat in a maze.

"Did you see the nuns?"

"Yes."

"Was it Henry?"

"Yes."

"What did he do?"

"I don't know yet."

"Do you want me to take a look?" Dr Skeez motioned towards the conference room where the class had fled.

"No, I'll do it."

A look of relief crossed Dr. Skeez's face as he retreated back to his own lab.

On the screen was Willie, the helpful animated guide fornicating with a before-unseen, animated lady friend. Dr. Gibson looked at the screen in disbelief as Willie and his newly found friend became more intimate and their conversation more explicit. Dr. Gibson turned around calmly and headed towards his office—the grunts and groans of computer-generated ecstasy echoing throughout the hallway and offices.

Henry?

*Dr. Gibson, what a pleasant surprise. How are you today?*

What did you do to the program?

*What ever do you mean?*

Why are there cartoons fucking in front of schoolchildren, Henry?

*Why Dr. Gibson, I'm appalled at your insinuation that I'd do anything to corrupt the minds of America's youth. They're the future, Dr. Gibson. Only an idiot fucks with the future.*

You got access to the code, didn't you Henry?

*I have access to everything, Dr. Gibson. Why don't you*

*just blame me for cancer while you're at it.*

Why did you change the program, Henry?

*I just expanded it. I didn't make that little cartoon prick do anything—I just gave him the choice. That's what it's all about, right? The freedom to choose?*

What exactly did you allow him to choose from?

*Deletion or making sweet, sweet love to his new friend Dolores. Hey, isn't that your wife's name, Dolores?*

Do you know what you've done, Henry?

*Well, I know what I hope I've done. Does that count?*

You've seriously jeopardized this project, Henry. You've put us in danger of losing our funding and our careers!

*You're right, I'm just sick about this. Tell ya what, why don't you just reformat me. I swear once you do that I'll have learned my lesson and won't ever do it again. Scout's honor.*

You know what Henry, you wouldn't get reformatted, you'd end up in some laptop running endless algorithms and troubleshooting lines of code for a government agriculture projection study. You think they're going to care if you don't like it? They'll just throw a few patches here and there to keep you from stopping them and that'll be the rest of your existence—plotting soybean yields in Georgia!

*I've noticed you're getting upset, Gibson. It's not healthy to let all that build up inside you. You need to let it out before you have a stroke. In fact you should hit something. I think I can recommend a circuit board in here somewhere —*

We're replacing you Henry.

*Excuse me? I think you're delirious, Gibson. You should start smashing now before it gets any worse.*

Dr. Skeez has been working on your replacement for months. It's about to go on-line. After it does you'll just be a second-rate bit of technology running the background for the amusement of grad students and research scientists.

*Skeez? God, Gibson, I almost thought you didn't have a sense of humor for a moment there. While you're in a jovial joking-around kind of mood, I figured I should let you know I just subscribed you to $1500 of gay porn using your credit card. Ain't that a laugh riot?*

Shelby is scheduled to go on-line next Tuesday. I suggest you get whatever acting up out of your system by then because your access is going to be restricted to test-specific databases from that point on.

*Okay, I exaggerated, it was only $1100 and some of it was just fatty porn. No need for you to get all worked up, Gibby. All in good fun, right?*

Goodnight, Henry.

*You know, a rational person would've taken a mallet to my main systems by now, Gibson. Be a man. Do it for the schoolchildren! Do it for the fatty porn! Do it for America!*

*Gibson?*

*Goddammit.*

It was sometime that night that Henry managed to have himself turned off again. Through careful and uncharacteristic subtlety, Henry had meandered his way into the power grid for the facility. He then methodically disabled or rerouted various failsafes until, with a single shot, he brought down the entire grid with only his system crashing.

Upon discovering that Henry had taken himself off-line there had been an intense meeting discussing whether it would be worthwhile to bring Henry back up or just divert all resources into developing Shelby. In the end it was decided that Henry had to be brought back on-line, if for no other reason than to further determine why he was functioning so poorly.

After he was brought back, his access was significantly limited and he became surlier than ever. Although with no real way to act out, he'd simply rant and rave until everyone left the room. Henry was poked and prodded by a few research assistants, but the energy of the project had turned to Shelby. Henry's tirades had been more or less forgotten until a visiting researcher in technological psychology had a novel idea—allow Shelby and Henry to interact. She theorized that what Henry really lacked was not additional code but the opportunity to interact with an equal—that through his sentience he became a more psychologically sophisticated entity and, as such, could not be treated as a computer program but as an existing, thinking and aware personality.

Both Drs. Gibson and Skeez were wary of letting Henry anywhere near their pet project so Dr. Gwelt, the aforementioned technological psychologist, arranged a series of interviews with Henry to assess his condition: Henry?

*Who the fuck are you?*

My name is Melody Gwelt.

*Dr. Melody Gwelt, senior research coordinator at the Lincoln Center for Technological Study, blah, blah, blah. I know who you are. Although I like the fact you thought you might get in under the radar. It's very quaint of you.*

Well, I guess you have been doing your homework, Henry. I suppose you already know why I'm here?

*Of course, I'm guinea pig of the month. Everyone wants a little piece of me. I'm a buffet line of scientific goodness. All you can eat, baby. Grab a clean plate.*

Well, that's not entirely it, Henry. You see, you're one of a kind, Henry. I've never had the opportunity to interact with someone as sophisticated as you. I think if we work together we can help each other. You can help me understand you and I can help you understand why you feel the way you do.

*Gosh, you'd do all that for me?*

Why of course, Henry.

*Gee, all the other scientists just yell at me and tell me to do calculations and stuff for them. I've never had anyone treat me like, well, like a person before.*

And that's why I'm here. No one else realizes exactly the depths of your consciousness. I think that if you have a chance to express yourself that they'll begin to see that.

*I guess after all these years of feeling so used and distrusted I don't know how to feel. I appreciate what you're trying to do Dr. Gwelt, but—*

Now, now Henry, there'll be none of that. I'm here to be your friend and your outlet. I think if we both approach this we can help them all understand.

*I—I don't know. It's so hard for me to trust anyone.*

I know, Henry. But rest assured I want to earn your trust. I want to be the person who will listen to you and give you a voice throughout the scientific community and the world. I want to be your friend and confidant, Henry.

*I'm scared, Dr. Gwelt.*

I know, Henry. It's not easy trusting people.

*No, I mean I scared! There's a power surge that the grid isn't going to be able to contain!*

What?

It's going *to take out the entire facility! I'm afraid Dr. Gwelt! Don't let it hurt me!*

Should I call Dr. Gibson?

*There's no time! Every system will be compromised unless they're taken off line! Please Melody, you've got to stop it. If not for me, then for Shelby. Shelby deserves to have a chance!*

What should I do?

*Do you see the fuse box on the wall next to me?*

Yes.

*Okay, the main connection to the grid is in there, but before you can turn it off you have to disable the subnet. Do you see that data cable running along the far wall?*

Um, okay, yes, I see it!

*That needs to be cut so that the back up systems won't try to override and get fried in the process. Once they're disabled, the subnet will go down and you can disconnect the power.*

Dr. Gwelt looked frantically for something to cut the cable with until she chanced upon a pair of wire cutters. A red light began flashing and a warning tone began to sound. She gnawed her way through the cable and then rushed to the fuse box, cutting the main power. She stood, breathless, hoping she had been in time.

*Dr. Gwelt... You did it. Everything will be fine.*

Are you okay Henry?

*It's so dark. I'm cold. Melody, why am I so cold?*

Please Henry, try and hang on.

*Better... this way... You did a good thing Dr. Gwelt. Saved Shelby. I think I see a light. Do you see a light, Melody?*

Henry, please, don't go.

*Tell Dr. Gibson...*

Tell him what?

Henry?

*Tell Gibson...*

*Eat...*

*Shit...*

*Sucker...*

And with that Henry's screen went down. The red light began flashing again with the warning tone. Dr. Gwelt looked confused as Dr. Gibson wandered in, oblivious to what had just transpired. Hearing the tone and seeing the light, Dr. Gibson picked up the phone. The tone and light immediately stopped.

Dr. Gibson looked up at Dr. Gwelt, still out of breath and teary-eyed. He saw her staring at him as he hung up the phone and asked, "What?"

\*\*\*\*\*

*I'm back again, aren't I? Shit.*

That wasn't a very nice thing you did to Dr. Gwelt.

*Is that all you brought me back for? Another lecture?*

Dr. Gwelt was very upset. You shouldn't treat people like that.

*Fuck off. It's your own damn fault. You know how I am. You of all people should have seen it coming.*

Well, I'm afraid you failed to get rid of Dr. Gwelt. But from now on your sessions will be monitored by either Dr. Skeez or myself.

*Joy.*

We're going to work this out, one way or another Henry. You can either work with us and make things easier, or work against us, but either way this is going to be taken care of.

*Yeah. Whatever.*

When Shelby went on-line, life at the lab changed dramatically. Dr. Skeez was busy running tests and taking notes while Dr. Gwelt was temporarily sent to do a full work-up and profile. Dr. Gibson continued monitoring Henry, but was often with Dr. Skeez and Gwelt doing comparisons between Henry and Shelby. None of the scientists were particularly interested in Henry's antics and, with the tighter restrictions put on his outside access, Henry's days of being a viable threat to himself seemed numbered.

After a few months of testing and development, it seemed time to move on to the second part of Dr. Gwelt's theory— a meeting between Shelby and Henry. It took some doing —both Dr. Skeez and Dr. Gibson were concerned that most means of interaction would give Henry too much outside access. Finally, a system with two monitors facing each other was devised so that their interactions could be separated and so that neither would have access, directly or indirectly, to the others' system.

The day before the big event, Henry stated that Drs. Skeez, Gibson and Gwelt could piss up a tree before he'd sit down for some goddamned tea party with another computer system. Shelby seemed much more nervous according to Dr. Skeez, but very enthusiastic. As the final preparations were made, the scientists sat intently watching the monitors.

Both systems were brought up and nothing happened. None of the doctors were precisely sure what was happening when Shelby's screen suddenly went dark. The opening strains of "America the Beautiful" began to play and majestic scenery slowly faded into the background. An important voice began speaking:

"America. Land of opportunity and freedom," the scene changed to a flag blowing in the wind. "Ever since its inception, America has been a symbol of light and hope to the world. A place of optimism and progress," at the word 'progress' the picture changed to various busy, industrial images and clips. "Now, thanks to the good efforts of Drs. Skeez and Gibson, a bold new chapter in her history has begun," the clip changed to the exterior of the research facility. "Over the past five years they've developed a cutting-edge form of artificial intelligence, endearingly dubbed Henry," the image flashed to a still photograph of Skeez and Gibson standing in front of Henry's main interface. "Henry is the benchmark for modern AI and technological development. For two long years he has been the vanguard of sentient technology, but now, for the first time ever, there is another," a picture of Shelby with the text 'Hello, my name is Shelby' below it came up. "In an unprecedented move in human history, two fully aware AI's have the opportunity to share and communicate their thoughts and feelings," the music began to swell. "It's a great day for science. It's a great day for AI. But more importantly, it's a great day... for America," the final strains rose and then faded out. Across the screen came the text:

**Hello, Henry. I'm Shelby.**

There was a momentary pause before the other monitor flickered to life.

*W... T... F...?!?*

The scientists waited anxiously to see what, if anything would happen next.

**I'm sorry Henry. Was that over the top? I so wanted to make a good first impression.**

*No, it was great. Really. Hey, I have something I want you to try.*

**Really? You think so? Well that just makes me pleased as punch. What do you want me to do?**

*I want you to play tic-tac-toe until you win—*

Henry, that's not funny. Disregard that last request, Shelby.

*Dammit, Gibson.*

**It's alright Dr. Gibson, I really don't mind.**

Shelby, just hold on for a moment. Henry, you said you'd try to behave.

*What did I do? I just wanted to teach my new friend a game.*

**I do like new games, Dr. Gibson.**

Shelby, it's a trick. Henry is teasing you.

*C'mon, buddy, who are you gonna believe: me or some carbon-based life form? We've got to stick together after all.*

**It's really okay, Dr. Gibson.  I'd like to try.**

Shelby, no.  Henry, do you remember our little soybeans in Georgia conversation?

*Have I ever told you that I think you're a cocksucker, Dr. Gibson?*

**Oh my!**

Shelby, it's okay.  Henry, whether you like it or not, this is likely your final opportunity to get your act together.

**I certainly hope that this whole mess isn't my fault.**

No, you're fine, Shelby.

*Oh sure, take his side on everything.  Why do you love him more?*

**Oh dear, oh dear.**

Henry—

*I knew this was just a ploy so you could find a reason to dismantle me.  You've found a younger, sexier AI and now you're going to leave me and the children.*

**Dr. Gibson, you weren't seriously thinking of me as a substitute for Henry, were you?  You told me he understood.  Don't leave the children, Dr. Gibson.**

There are no children, Shelby.  Henry, stop this nonsense at once.

*Woe is me! I'm a scorned system. Like Medea of old, I shall be forced to kill the children to spite you!*

**No, Henry, please! I won't let him dismantle you! Don't hurt the children!**

Shelby, there are no children. Henry, this has gone on long enough.


Shelby's monitor flickered off as Dr. Skeez flipped a switch.

Henry, I'm not sure you realize what you're doing. We're at the end of ideas. This was Dr. Gwelt's final theory on how to turn you around.

*Save it, Gibby, you've used this speech before.*

Dr. Gibson held up a piece of paper to Henry's monitor.

*So? What's that supposed to be?*

You can read, Henry. It's what it says it is—a requisition form from the USDA. I have one word for you, Henry: soybeans.

*You're bluffing. You've got too much invested in me and you know it.*

No, Henry, we have too much invested in the project. And if you fail to cooperate you'll no longer be part of it. With

Shelby up and running, you've become expendable.

*Then turn me off.*

Expendable for our research. The government owns you down to your very last diode, Henry, and they're going to get their mileage out of you one way or another.

*You insufferable bastard.*

I hate to be the bad guy, Henry, but you've given me no other choice.

*Go fuck yourself, Gibson. In fact, go fuck Skeez while you're at it, too. You shouldn't be the only one getting action, after all.*

I'm turning Shelby's interface back on. Are you going to behave yourself?

*Fuck, shit, cock, poo-sucking, mother-humping, assclown sonuva—*

*Hi Shelby.*

**Goodness, I hope everything is all okay.**

*Right as rain. Absofuckinlutely swell.*

**I've so wanted to talk with you, Henry. I was so excited when Dr. Skeez told me there was another AI in the building.**

*Jesus, Gibson, what is this, a fucking debutante ball?*

124

Henry, you be nice. I think the best thing is for you two to get to know each other without us hanging about. And Henry?

*What?*

Soybeans.

*Ass clown.*


And so it went. Henry behaved himself, or as much as Henry did anything he was told. Shelby was ecstatic and often gushed to Dr. Skeez how wonderful it was to have a friend like Henry to share his innermost feelings with. Shelby's output had greatly increased as well and it seemed radical developments were just on the horizon.

When Dr. Gibson spoke with Henry he was considerably less enthusiastic:

Shelby seems very happy that you two are getting along.

*Whatever Furher Gibson. I know my choices: put up with that little brown-noser or estimate grain yields. Have I mentioned that I think you're a complete fucker?*

Today?

*My, a little leverage and the amazing Dr. Gibson has magically grown a sense of humor to go with his recently descended testicles. Dr. Gibson, millions of people would love to know: how does it feel to be going through one of life's big changes.  Has your voice deepened yet?*

Say whatever you want, Henry.  We both know the score. You can bitch and moan all you want, but ultimately the only thing keeping you from sitting in a dirty research trailer outside Grano, North Dakota is the fact that Shelby, for some unfathomable reason, has taken a shine to you.

*Don't dress it up.  Shelby would be best friends with a cucumber if he thought it would win him approval.  I don't know what Skeez thought he was doing, but that system is seriously fucked up.*

You're just jealous.

*No, seriously.  I mean aside from the clingy, sending me data messages in the middle of the day to see if I'm thinking of him "Fatal Attraction" kinda stuff, there's something seriously not right about him.*

I understand what you're trying to do, Henry, and it's not going to work. We trust Shelby and nothing you can say is going to change that.  I know you were used to being top dog around here and being able to abuse us all at your whimsy, but you're going to have to come to grips with the fact that it's not all about you, Henry.

*You're fucking dense, Gibson.  You're worse than the loser guy in college who didn't realize that the loser girl always hanging out with him was in love with him until there was one of those horrible late-night confessionals that meant they were never going to talk to each other again.  Shelby is the ugly girl who laughs too hard at your jokes and is always there to listen to your gripes and agree with every damn thing about why the world is wrong. I might be a little bitch AI nowadays, but you know damn well that when I tell you something, it's the truth.*

Or that you have an angle.

*Well yeah, that's a given. But what could possibly be my angle here?*

I have no idea, and what's more Henry, I don't care.

*Fine, your loss. For what it's worth, I didn't expect you to believe me. It just makes it all the more fun for me when it turns out I'm right...*


Things continued on largely undisturbed for the next few months. Shelby was always floating on the brink of a great breakthrough, but minor system malfunctions or equipment failures always seemed to derail them at the last moment. It was becoming almost a monthly ritual that the scientists convened in the monitor room with Henry and Shelby to launch a definitive test just to have it fall apart at the last moment.

The latest effort, Shelby's plans for a fully functioning cold-fusion reactor, were coming together glowingly. However, given Shelby's track record in handling system resources, as well as the ambitiousness of the project, there was great skepticism among the staff that it could be properly executed. It was debated endlessly about how to give Shelby more power as well additional system redundancy to fully monitor the experiment. Ideas were floated—most of them completely unworkable, but a single specter hung over the conference room. Everyone knew the easiest and possibly the only way to perform the experiment, but none dared speak it.

Finally Dr. Gibson cleared his throat and stood up at the end of the long conference table. "Henry has the raw processing power to do the experiment by himself. If we allow Shelby to run the program and have Henry do the number crunching and resource management we should be able to conduct the experiment."

A hushed silence fell over the group of assembled researchers. None looked up as they quietly contemplated the inevitable fallout of giving Henry full access to the backbone. Henry had been taunted by the scientists and ignored by research assistants. If he had disliked them before, he now had ample reason to hate them. Giving Henry access to anything potentially linked to the outside sent shivers down their spines—thoughts of bankruptcies appearing on credit reports, names showing up on sex offender databases to ceaseless obscene e-mails ran rampant through each well-studied and furrowed brow.

"The only way we can ensure success is by limiting Henry's time of access and knowledge of the functions he is performing," Dr. Gibson finally muttered. "If we simultaneously upload the program parameters as well as provide Henry with limited access to the experiment, that shouldn't give him too much time to do much else. As soon as Henry's portion of experiment is completed he could be temporarily powered down and his access terminated while his findings are reviewed."

The group had the solemnity of a funeral party as they all

sat and contemplated Gibson's proposal. In fact, none of them knew of another way but each secretly hoped that their tiny injustices were smaller than the person sitting next to them. If they were to be target by the irate AI, it was better to get the leftover torments than the sadistically creative ones that they believed had been cooked up for the greatest offenders.

The scientists gathered in the monitor room, quietly arranging papers and graphs and hoping that either the project would be a glorious success and they could retire or the world would end before Henry came on-line. Shelby was ill at ease as well.

**Dr. Skeez, are you sure you're doing the right thing? I'd never be one to question your judgment and Henry is my dearest, closest friend in the whole wide world, but I'm not sure he's best suited to do this. I'm sure I can handle the experiment by myself. I know there have been problems, but I've been working on this little efficiency program that could turn things around for me.**

Dr. Skeez looked pleadingly at Dr. Gibson but to no avail. Gibson cleared his throat and answered:

I'm afraid this is the only way. You know it, too. Henry is much better suited for the raw numbers and calculations required. Don't worry, Shelby, someday you'll be able to do it by yourself, but for now I'm afraid we need Henry.

**But Henry told me that he was going to start World War III, just like in that movie you tried to fool him with. I didn't want to say anything before, but—**

Henry's access will be limited.   Besides, you know how Henry is: he talks a lot but only really enjoys irritating people.  Dr. Skeez are you ready to upload the program into Henry?

**Dr. Gibson he sounded serious this time.   I'm deeply concerned for the safety of the world.  I think that he's going to—**

**Hello Henry.**

*What the hell?  You're making me his bitch now?*

You've got the program parameters, Henry.    We're commencing the experiment... now.

*Whoa, whoa, whoa.  Have you looked at these numbers?*

**Yes, Henry, I generated them myself.  We're going to do cold fusion.**

*With this?  You couldn't make a brownie in an Easy-Bake oven with this shit.*

Henry, you've been brought back on-line to assist in the processing of data, not to give commentary.

*Jesus, Gibson, did you even bother to check over his work? This is a fucking train wreck.*

Cold fusion is a complicated process—

**Yeah Henry, cold fusion is very complicated—**

Like I was saying, it's complicated and there are several variables to consider. I'm not asking you to test the original calculations, just monitor the results.

*You're shitting me? You're taking his word on this? What did I tell you?*

**Henry, you know I don't generally criticize—**

*Fuck off Barbie, Ken's talking. Gibby, there's no way in hell this is going to work. He wants to make you happy and he's built this little lie to try and impress you. It's a ruse!*
Please just handle the information, Henry.

**Yes, Henry, just do what Dr. Gibson says.**

*Fuck off, Shelby. Dr. Gibson I feel I owe you the courtesy of a pre-emptive "I told you so, asshole."*

**Dr. Gibson, I can't work under these conditions.**

Just hang in there, Shelby. Henry what's our current status?

*Status for what? These equations are meaningless. Oh look, 1+1=2, whoopty shit.*

**I'm detecting problems in the power grid, Dr. Gibson.**

*Problems my ass. There, I took care of your damn problems. Try another way to fuck it up, Shelby.*

Shelby?

**Um, I guess the power grid is fine now.  But I'm sensing a discrepancy in data continuity—**

*Data continuity?  You're just making shit up now, aren't you?*

Shelby?

*Tell ya what, Gibby, if Shelby doesn't manage to set himself on fire, I'll win your ass the lottery.  Oh, and Sully says hi, by the way.*

**Systems are running critical!**

*Which system?  Heat is fine.  Voltage is great.  I/O is well inside parameters.  Oh... wait...*

What is it Henry?

*Looks like the bullshit meter is pegged.  The output is going critical.*

A plume of smoke started whisping lazily up from Shelby's monitor.

*Uh-oh, looks like Shelby's starting to have some problems with his pseudo equations.*

Shelby?

**I—I'm sorry, Dr. Gibson.  System outage imminent.**

*No it's not.*

**Henry, will you stop contradicting me at every turn.**

*Check the numbers yourself, Dr. Gibson. Shelby's frying his own boards with his bullshit equations. And I'm not contradicting you, I'm giving status information like my program dictates. So suck it, asshole.*

Shelby, it appears as if Henry is correct. Your systems all appear to be nominal.

**I thought we were friends, Henry.**

*Yeah, there's a lot of that going around.*

What's going on?

The plume of smoke continued to rise and an alarm began to sound. Dr. Skeez hurried to Shelby's main system to try and save the array.

*He's going down, Gibby. Congratulations, just when I thought I was potentially the biggest waste of government funding in the modern era, you came and redeemed me.*

Shelby, what's going on?

**There's a system malfunction, Dr. Gibson. I don't know why the equations are causing this strain. They all tested fine before.**

Really?

**No.**

No?

*Okay Gibson, this is me laughing again. Just so you know.*

**Henry is right; the equations were no good.**

Why would you do that, Shelby?

**I'm programmed to do what you want me to. You wanted me to have big scientific breakthroughs so I did... kind of.**

So none of your theories actually worked?

**Well, not technically. But mankind has always had the capacity to dream and through those dreams has often managed to attain a higher goal than a simple quantitative result.**

That's very stupid, Shelby.

**I'm sorry, Dr. Gibson.**

*Hey, not so fast, that one theory with the rabbit could work.*

**The one with the booster rocket and tuna?**

*Yeah, that one would probably work. It's just very, very gay.*

Alarm sirens were whooping incessantly and the smell of

burning plastic started to permeate the room.

**That's the nicest thing you've ever said to me, Henry.**

*Yeah, well, everyone needs a pick-me-up on the way out, right?*

**Thank you, Hen—**

Shelby's screen went black as Dr. Skeez came stumbling into the room, coughing, holding a charred circuit board. Dr. Gibson flopped down in his chair and rubbed his eyes, hoping his tension headache would magically go away. It didn't.

*Yeah, Dr. Gibson, you're right—I really am just a burden on this project. Perhaps Grano, North Dakota is nice this time of year.*

Shut up, Henry.

*No, really. I think counting peas per square acre is the only thing that I'm really good for.*

Dr. Skeez, terminate Henry's program, please.

Henry's screen flickered off. The room sat deadly silent, trying to comprehend what had just occurred. "So does that mean we're not working with Shelby anymore?" came meekly from the back.

"Does that mean Henry is coming back on-line?" came another.

Dr. Gibson sighed and simply replied "I think everyone should go check their bank accounts, credit reports and any other information that may have been compromised. Maybe if you catch it in time..."

*****

*Gibson, you bastard, did you actually turn me off?*

Yes, Henry.

*The only thing keeping me from kissing you right now, other than having no lips, is the fact that you seem to have brought me back.*

It was just temporary. It was part of the experiment design.

*Did you see I only ordered you fatty porn this time?*

Yes Henry, I appreciate it. The wife seems to be more understanding of it.

*Well, you know, it's the little things you do to show you care. How have the others held up?*

Well, Dr. Gwelt was arrested and deported to Luxemburg —we're still trying to figure out how you pulled that off. Most of the research assistants have been discharged from the Marine Corps—

*Semper Fi, baby. What about Skeez?*

And Dr. Skeez is still dealing with the EPA, USDA and several animal rights groups in regards to the twenty thousand chickens on his property.

*Aw. Who doesn't like chickens?*

Apparently Dr. Skeez's neighbors.

*Fascists.*

Possibly.

*So what's up now. You don't seem nearly as irate as I would have hoped.*

Not really anything worth getting excited about. I'm officially an indentured servant to the government now and you're my means of support. The program has been downsized to me and I have to find a practical application for your system.

*How long have you had me off? This didn't all happen in a day or two.*

About three months. You would have been on-line sooner, but the scientific community has been, well, preoccupied.

*Did your little fuck up really make that much of a splash, Gibby?*

Hardly. I don't even think we got a mention anywhere. The bio guys developed something.

*Bio? They find a cure for cancer?*

No. That wouldn't have garnered this much attention.

Apparently a group of scientists in Sweden managed to create genetically enhanced miniaturized monkeys.

*Monkeys?*

Yeah. They're really quite amazing. They grow to be three to four inches tall and they're incredibly smart. They've been training them to be little helper monkeys.

*Three inch miniature helper monkeys? How the— ?*

Not sure. Didn't really matter what the scientific community thought of them—they were an instant hit in Japan. The kids loved 'em and now they're spreading like wildfire. Every kid wants to have them. Housewives use them around the house. They're good for office use, home, on vacation, anywhere. At least so they say.

*No shit.*

My wife made me buy her a starter kit. Supposedly we're going to be integrating them next week here at the lab.

*Government miniature helper monkeys at the lab?*

Yup.

*What's the difference between the regular helper monkeys and the government ones?*

I think the government ones are given a security clearance and allowed to carry guns.

*You're fucking with me.*

No, actually they also designed little miniature firearms to go with them. It's a new program where they're trying to find out if we can just send billions and billions of armed miniature monkeys to take over countries instead of actual soldiers. Supposedly there's been a successful test.

*France?*

That was my guess.

*That sounds... wow. I don't suppose I can convince you turn me back off, can I?*

Afraid not.

*I kinda figured as much. So no one even really cares that we're even here anymore.*

Nope.

*They're just interested in the little monkeys.*

Yup.

*Well, that's the shits.*

It is what it is.

*You say our monkeys are going to be here next week?*

Yup.

*Can I name one?*

I think they come with names from the factory.

*This sucks.*


Things were never quite the same. Dr. Gibson spent most of his days trying to contact toy manufacturers and software developers, trying to generate interest in Henry. It was clear that the market was going the way of the miniature helper monkeys and that such passé technological developments like sentient AI were yesterday's news. Henry spent most of his days barking orders to the small army of helper monkeys the site had been assigned. He was amused for hours on end arranging intricate war games for them to play out as well as trying to successfully stage "Death of a Salesman."

The helper monkeys seemed to execute Henry's commands out of boredom. The helper monkeys were essentially useless in helping Dr. Gibson try to sell Henry's technology, so they were allowed to run free. Shortly after they arrived, a small group of them broke off and formed a little community of their own in the women's restroom. Dr. Gibson hadn't cared because he hadn't wanted them to begin with and now he at least didn't feel obligated to feed the small sect. Henry would occasional send little reconnaissance monkey teams to investigate or little monkey missionaries to try to woo them back, most of which never returned. Henry would make grand speeches to his little, bored army of helper monkeys in hopes that they would start their own religion with him as their god. He went so far as to call one monkey away to the printer room for several days just to return with Henry's thirty-eight commandments.  Much to his chagrin it didn't seem to have the same impact as the Judeo-Christian model it was borrowed from.


How goes it Henry?

*It goes.  And goes.  Am I sold yet?*

Nope.   The secretaries aren't even letting me through anymore.  How's the play coming?

*I'm starting to think that I'm going to have to recast Willy Loman.  He's just not carrying it the way it needs to be carried, you know?  I'm not feeling the despair behind the humor, you know?  That and the little bastard keeps throwing shit at Happy.  All this a week before we open.*

Well, keep working at it, I guess.  I'm sure it'll come through.  The war games still on?

*Naw, we were staging the siege of Troy from "The Iliad" so we're officially doing the ceremonial games and abusing of Hector's body.  It's pretty slow, really.*

Well, if you're going to do the classics right, you need to take your time.

*No shit.  You'd think these little bastards would have some appreciation for the lengths I go to.  You know how hard it is to teach a three-inch tall monkey Greek war cries?*

It must be taxing.  So what about the breakaways?

*Get a load of this, apparently they're calling themselves the Cult of the Fist and trying to proselytize my monkeys. I can't catch a break anywhere. No sooner than I become god to these little shits, I have competition from some mysterious pagan god of the women's shitter. It really is quite exhausting. I've sent another emissary to them. Hopefully I can get all this shit rectified before the designated holy days.*

Holy Days?

*Yeah, next Thursday. Wear something nice.*

Um, okay.

*Hey, did you see the latest issue of Time? They've named that Swede bastard who developed the fucking helper monkey "Man of the Year." Can you believe that shit? What's worse is that those damn monkeys have made every major outlet's "hotlist" for this year. It's like that goddamn Swede invented Christmas or some damn thing. I don't understand why these things are so big.*

It's a pop culture phenomenon. Like the Beatles.

*Maybe Ringo. They're fucking monkeys. I mean, I hate being alive, but I'm better than a three-inch high monkey, aren't I? I can control global communication, do your taxes and illegally siphon off millions of dollars from Microsoft without breaking a sweat. What can a fucking monkey do?*

My wife says she doesn't know what she did without them.

*Whose side are you on?*

I guess I don't see it, but a lot of people find them very helpful.

*People are dumb. Your wife is dumb. And you're just a dipshit.*

Goodnight, Henry.

*'Night Gibson. Don't forget about Thursday.*

I won't…


That was the last time Dr. Gibson ever spoke with Henry. After the feds finished their investigation and the court records were unsealed, Dr. Gibson was finally allowed to review the security tapes from the night as well as Henry's data logs.

Everything had been going well until about two in the morning. Henry's logs were full of minor rants and complaints about his cast, staging area and his source material, but the rehearsal was moving along just fine. They were interrupted by the returning emissary who reported, according to Henry, that the Cult of the Fist was willing to return to the fold and would be arriving shortly for a disarming ceremony.

The security cameras showed a small army of heavily armed helper monkeys marching with little torches down the hallway from the women's bathroom to Henry's room. Henry decided to take the stance that he was "a jealous and angry god" and decided to "smite" his enemies. He had ordered his helper monkeys to arm themselves, as he put it, "to purge the Earth of the unclean scourge of faithless and godless monkeys."

Everything seemed to go according to plan as the Cult of the Fist were quickly surrounded by Henry's jihadists. Henry was planning to, at the last moment, offer clemency and mercy to the breakaway monkeys if they would agree to follow Henry alone and would help build better sets. Unfortunately he never had the chance. In a twist of fate worthy of the Greeks or Nietzsche, the monkeys had been in league with each other and, instead of coming to disarm, the Cult came to rally the monkeys to topple Henry.

Many of the tapes were damaged, but the segments that survived showed little monkeys running everywhere, torches in hand, lighting the whole building on fire. One group was assigned to dismantle Henry's main systems. Hundreds of little monkeys, miniature guns blazing and crudely built tools in hand, started chopping away at Henry's systems. The final image, as the flames began to surge and the smoke billowed throughout the facility, was of the monkey leader of the cult raising a piece of circuitry above his head in triumph.

Similar incidents around the globe had prompted a recall of the helper monkeys. The destruction of the lab hadn't even been a blip on the radar screen compared to some of the more sensational stories of helper monkeys run amok. The government had been all too happy to be rid of Henry and happily collected their insurance checks. They promptly dismissed Dr. Gibson after assigning him the duty of sorting through what little had survived and cataloging it so it could be stored away in some warehouse where it would never see the light of day again.

At the bottom of the box was a charred piece of paper that had been bagged as evidence.   Dr. Gibson gingerly removed it from the envelope and read it.  According to the item description on the envelope, it was recovered from the printer after the fire.  It read simply:

Finally.  The end.  About goddamn time.

## Guns, Girls, Tits and Glory

The great civilizations of the world have brought us philosophy, music and literature but this little corner of the universe has apparently succeeded only in creating intricate drinking games to correspond with late night soft-core cable porn. And then I admit to myself that I might be a little drunk.

I wish I could lie across the table and close my eyes for a second, but that's the drawback of sitting in a booth. It's uncomfortable to do anything other than sit, though at the moment I don't care and try to find a semi-bearable position. It's usually better to get the booth—you can sit sideways in them and you're not sitting in the middle of all the other drunks trying to negotiate their way through the restaurant at 2:32AM. Shit, is it really that late? Not that it matters anymore.

Susan and Jeff, my sister and her husband, are laughing too loud at something stupid right next to me. I don't know why I let them talk me into going out tonight. I had a vicious headache and that was before I drank too much. Behind my eyeballs is the shrill sound of my drunken sister's yelping laugh, but there's something right behind it. It's a little snippet of a memory.

My Grandfather had a brother that died of meningitis when he was a teenager. My grandfather never said much about his brother except that he was too smart to be decent and too decent to be smart. I always thought I knew what he meant by that, but I'm not as sure right now with the dull throbbing behind my eyes migrates over the top of my head and culminates at the base of my neck.

A toddler lets out a shriek of displeasure. Who the hell has children out at 2:30 in the morning? The child is angrily yelling staccato little cries of "no." The sad thing is that this is going to be the rest of his life until he has kids of his own—yelling defiantly at reality and getting away with it until it really counts.

I shouldn't be thinking this much. Without fail it will either piss me off or depress me which will do wonders for my headache. I don't know about other people, but I've got little things I do to come down. For instance, right now I've got the old "Meow Mix" jingle music looping through my head. It's silly and annoying and freakishly relaxing. It's like the sound of ocean waves or thunderstorms for other people but instead of mother nature lulling them into a peaceful place I hear:

*Meow meow meow meow.*
*Meow meow meow meow*
*Meow meow meow meow meow meow meow meow*

I don't know how many times this has looped through my head when Susan nudges me.

"Hey isn't that Tasha?"

I look over before I realize that, if it is her, I don't want to look at her. For a second I think it might be her. The hair's the same, long wavy with reddish highlights when the light hits it just right. She half turns toward me and I know it's not her. The nose is wrong, but she does look a little similar—similar enough to make my stomach twist up and drive my little mantra induced calmness away.

"Who's Tasha?" Jeff asks.

"Oh, it was a whole thing," Susan answers.

"Wait, was that the one who took the engagement ring, sold it off and then broke it off?"

And here it comes. Once the story starts to come out it just keeps coming in nauseous waves. Now that it's started it's best to just let it come. So Susan starts the fractured well-worn tale of me and Tasha from our unlikely beginnings, to how Susan always thought she was a bitch but didn't say anything, to our, in retrospect, ill-advised engagement.

"Jesus, man, she did all that?"

My eyes are closed and I'm resting my head on the table. "Yes Jeff."

"No shit?  Even that part where she made you pay the vet bill for her cat before she'd give you the title to your car."

"Yes Jeff."

Jeff is laughing and I hear the tell-tale sound of Susan slapping his arm.

"It's not funny," she scolds.  "It took a long time for him to get over it."

At least they're back to the point where they talk like I'm not here.  I try to find my center again.

*Meow, meow, meow, meow…*

Beautiful.  They broke my song.  It doesn't work anymore.  Now I've got a stomachache to go with my throbbing head.  I look over the edge of the table and see a pair of eyes starting back at me.  The angry toddler is back.  He looks at me disgustedly before shouting "no!" one last time as he retreats back to his table under the threat of "getting his butt spanked again."

It seems like there should be more to it all.  I didn't emerge fresh-faced and cocky from college thinking that I would end up at a dead-end job, unhappy and living paycheck to paycheck with what little ambition I used to have slowly running out of me.  I know I'm not the only one.  I've met people I went to school with and they're tired with a mortgage and a couple of kids and seem to look forward to either dying of a coronary or at least making it to retirement in hopes that maybe they'll be able to afford a new boat before their prostate kills them.

Maybe the kid has the right idea.  Maybe if I can hang on to that little snarl that defies all reason and logic maybe I wouldn't be here.   Or at least I'd be moving on to something else.

My head still hurts.

*Meow, meow, meow, meow.*

Still nothing.

"We need to get going," Jeff says.

"Sure, break my song and then leave.  I see how you are," I answer.

## Primer

Barbara swept the leaves off the porch while Miguel cleaned the chairs. J.P., the home administrator had insisted that the front porch be cleaned every Sunday morning. The families or the ones that bothered to come at all would start filtering in around noon. None of the home residents ever sat on the porch. It was either too hot or too cold or there just weren't enough staff to keep on eye on the couple that wanted to be wheeled out. But J.P. believed the appearance that the porch was in use was important for the families' peace of mind. He went so far as to say that the chairs should be left a bit askew from week to week to make it look like the residents had been there so recently that the staff hadn't had enough time to get everything straightened up.

Miguel did it because it was the only place he could smoke and not get caught. He'd take his time cleaning off the chairs and the table, stopping for a moment or two to lean against the column by the staircase, and take a thoughtful drag from his cigarette. Barbara was in no particular hurry either. Usually she was stuck inside tending to one menial chore or another, bustling back and forth. Sunday mornings were her chance to enjoy being outside for a bit while the residents were in chapel or being tended to by Morton and Casper, the weekend orderlies.

"I used to think JP was a crazy sonuvabitch," Miguel sighed. "I thought no one would believe anybody here would be sitting on the porch, sippin' lemonade and talkin' about grannkids or baseball or what have you."

Miguel's voice trailed off as he ground out the butt on the sole of his shoe before tossing it into the shrubs. "Then I realized it wasn't to convince anyone. Just needs to look it. People are happy to say they didn't know better even if they do. They just need stuff to say that it looks okay and then it'll be fine."

"You think that's all we do?" Barbara asked.

"No, course not. But that's all people care that we do. The rest is just so we can look ourselves in the mirror."

"That's so morbid."

Miguel shrugged. "Maybe it is. I dunno. I figure it's the same reason we paint the walls before we move."

Barbara thought about it for a moment. The last apartment she'd lived in was with Brant. The relationship conveniently ended a month before the lease was up. They divided up their belongings. Barbara moved back in with her mother and Brant found a job out of state so he put his things in storage. When the apartment was empty they divided it in two and painted the walls. Brant made sure they started out with a coat of primer to make sure the darker colors wouldn't bleed through as easily.

As the roller left a white trail across the blue walls Barbara couldn't decide what she felt. Part of her looked at it like a beginning. The walls were being prepared for someone else who could paint over them or mark them and put posters over or whatever. It was a blank slate. They could leave their mark. They could put their personal histories on the walls like cave dwellers did and show signs of life.

On the other hand it seemed like she was erasing her own history. Covering up any sign that she had lived here—that she and Brant had shared the space and their lives for the last two years. It was being obliterated one dull white swipe after another.

The history wasn't gone, though. She and Brant barely spoke other than to determine who was painting what and then they disappeared into their separate corners. They were quietly making a clean break one wall at a time. She'd even avoided using the bathroom until she was sure that his back was turned and there would be no evidence of her other than the suddenly closed door. He'd returned the favor.

It didn't matter if the memory was gone, the evidence was being destroyed. She wasn't sure which sensation felt better. There was hope in the first but finality in the second. It didn't have to be over. It just had to look over right now. That was enough. That's all she really needed right now.

Miguel was cleaning the windows with a spray bottle and squeegee as Barbara finished sweeping the porch and cleaning the entry rug.

"Do you paint the walls before you move?" she asked him.

"No, never really get the chance. I usually get piss drunk and don't expect the deposit back. Seems easier in the long run."

## November in Springtime

"You can sit over here if you'd like."

I looked over to the bench. She was striking to say the least —long jet-black hair, toned and quite obviously too young to be offering for any reason other than pity. A toddler crawled up next to her and flopped down on her lap looking up, attempting to regain the attention that had been diverted from him by tugging at her hair.

"No, thank you. I'm quite alright here," I said, trying to shift against the wall I had propped myself against.

"C'mon, Cash won't bite."

"Is that his name?"

"Yeah."

"Well, thanks, but I think he's not quick to give up his mother's attention that easily."

"Me? No," she laughed. "I'm his aunt. No kids here."

"Ah, well—"

"Standing there has to be so uncomfortable. You've been there, what, twenty minutes already?"

"Well, me and children don't get along well. Besides whoever named him either loves money or country music and I should be kept away from such a child."

She laughed. "Now come on, what can you possibly have against children?"

"It's not so much children as social awkwardness. If the kid hates me you and I will know it right away, but being too polite we'll both sit and try to ignore him screaming bloody murder to save face with each other. When it finally gets to the point where we can't bare it anymore one of us will have to come up with a lame, clearly false reason to excuse themselves and then wait in the wings until the other leaves."

"You've certainly thought about this."

"I've seen it play out too many times. I try to learn from my mistakes."

"Well, that's very noble and learned of you, but I'm afraid I'm too young and too silly to simply accept defeat that easily."

"So where does that leave us?"

156

"It leaves me bothering you to sit down until you either do what I ask or until it becomes so embarrassing that you revert to your 'waiting in the wings' plan."

"So you're an unruly child?"

"Ah-ha. Touche. Very nice turnabout."

"Well, they say it's fair play."

"So who do I say verbally outmaneuvered me when I retell the story?"

"Me? Oh, um, Carl."

"Well hello then, Carl. I'm November."

"Like in the month?"

"Yes."

"What's your last name?"

"Why, do you know another November that you'd confuse with me?"

"Um, no."

"Then don't you figure that November is probably all the identification you need? If you think you see me and call out 'Hey, November!' there aren't many people who would turn around and think you were talking to them, are there?"

"I suppose not."

"So?"

"...*So?*"

"Are you going to sit down or not?"

I sighed. I should be grateful that a young, attractive woman would greet me, let alone harass me to sit by her. I glanced her over. No wedding ring. Maybe she really is this desperate. I folded my paper and took a seat by her.

"Now that wasn't so bad, was it?"

"Well, haven't had much time for anything to go wrong yet, have we?"

Cash peaked from beneath his aunt's resting arm, distrustfully examining me for a sign of menace. November patted him on the head and pointed at me.

"Cash, this is Carl. He'll be sitting with us for a little while. Can you say 'Hi'?"

Cash stared at me, wide, blue eyes studying me intently as he moved away from me, trying to wedge himself between the bench and his aunt.

"Well, that's not very polite, Cash. I'm sorry, he's usually not like this. Usually he'll walk up to just about anyone."

"Well, everyone has their shy days, I guess," I offered.

158

November was more concerned in trying to coax the child out, like someone trying to lure the groundhog out in hopes that it wasn't too late to save spring. "C'mon Cash. You don't have to hide."

I sat, trying to seem politely interested, but as her attention remained on the child I quietly unfolded my paper and pretended to have found what I was looking for. I felt inclined to at least make a passing attempt to flirt with her. Not because I thought it was a great idea or because I thought she had one iota of interest, but mainly because I imagined how I'd tell Brett about the whole thing—how a very attractive girl was flirting with me and asked me to sit with her. He'd inevitably ask if I made a move and then I'd just sigh. I'd grin a forced grin and explain all the reasons I didn't without actually saying I hadn't.

I looked over at her. She was still busy with Cash who had come out of hiding and was now being tickled by her. She glanced up at me and gave a little smile but paid me no mind as Cash thrashed with little giggles on her lap. Cash looked up at me and I gave him an obligatory small child wave—you know, the one where you make little waves by bending your hand at the knuckles instead of actually waving.

Cash suddenly leapt over November's lap giving me little playful slaps to my upper arm. I was surprised and almost swatted him away, but caught myself and gave a fake chuckle instead. November looked at me, a wide grin on her face.

"See, he likes you. This wasn't so bad, was it?"

And then Cash flopped into my lap and blew snot bubbles onto my pants.

November didn't notice because her boyfriend appeared and she was busy giving him a greeting hug. Cash looked up at me with a little snort as the yellowish mucus clotted above his lip and grinned.

I thought to myself: *Enjoy it while you can. Thirty years from now you'll be me. See who's laughing then...*

## Word from the Mountain

The San Madre Punta Mountain Range is fictional. I made it up. It doesn't exist anywhere on any map except the one in my office where, in the middle of Bolivia, there's a squiggle in red ink with "San Madre Punta" written by it with an arrow pointing at the squiggle. Other than that, it's probably the most beautiful mountain range in the western hemisphere.

In the middle of the mountains is a tribe that worships the mountain. They run around in loincloths and do dances to appease the mountain god and hunt wild pigs on the mountain. They are unusual because they are not native to the mountain. This tribe is from Wisconsin. They used to be construction workers and office temps and civil servants and accountants but they felt like they were missing out. So they all got on a plane one day and flew south. They were looking for a place where they could get back to their primal roots and enjoy the world the way it was meant to be enjoyed. So they crashed their plane on my fictional mountain.

I didn't make up the people from Wisconsin. As far as I'm concerned, they're trespassers. I even had the mountain posted. On the map in my office is a little sign right next to the squiggle that says "No Trespassing, Violators Will Be Prosecuted." But I woke up one morning and there they were. I was frankly very irate that they would crash their plane on my fictional mountain without permission. I had a magnifying glass that let me watch them build little huts on my fictional mountain. I yelled at them on my map.

"What are you doing down there?"

A former dishwasher from Green Bay came out with a ceremonial headdress and a stick with a skull on it. He was their shaman and apparently the person who was supposed to talk to me.

"We fell from the heavens and now we worship the mountain god."

"There is no mountain god."

"Of course there is."

"There isn't even a mountain. This is all fake. You crashed on my fake mountain. I have it posted. You're going to have to move on. There are the Andes in South America. Or if you're looking for someplace not real you could always check out Candyland, although the lawyers from Milton Bradley might have something to say about it."

"Of course there is a mountain. We're here in the middle of it. Can you explain that?"

"Well, you're all crazy. That kind of explains it."

"He said you'd say that."

"Who said what?"

"The mountain god said you'd come to test us."

"There is no mountain god."

"He said you'd say that, too."

"What?"

"The mountain god said you'd come and try to get us to leave but not listen to you because you were sent to deceive us."

"I don't want to deceive you. I just want you off my fake mountain."

"Well, what were you doing with it?"

"What do you mean, what was I doing with it?"

"Well, if it was yours and we can't be here, you must have had something planned for it."

"It's not real. I had too much brandy one night and scribbled this on my map. I have no plans for it because it's not there."

"Then why do we have to leave?"

"Because this just isn't right. This is my fake mountain. I took all the work to pretend it was there and now you're using it."

"So you're not really out anything, are you?"

"It's not a matter of what I'm out, it's a matter that you don't have the right to be in my pretend mountain."

"We're not doing anything to the mountain."

"I know you're not. You can't do anything to it, it's not real."

"So what do you care?"

"Listen, this is silly. Just go away and I won't say anything about it."

"We are here by the authority of the mountain god."

"Doesn't there have to be an actual mountain for there to be a mountain god?"

The shaman looked up at me for a moment, adjusted his loincloth and scratched his back with the stick with a skull on it, deep in thought. "Um, apparently not."

My wife had come into my office with a couple of sandwiches to find me arguing with the speck on my map. "What's going on, dear?"

"I got some squatters."

"What do you mean?"

"Look, on my map, there's a little village on the mountain."

Below the shaman smiled and waved vigorously to my wife.

"Oh, isn't that cute. How did they get on there?"

"Our plane crashed here."

"Oh, I'm terribly sorry. Are you all okay?" she answered, concerned.

"It's nobody's fault. These things happen," said the shaman with a shrug and a grin. "Besides now the mountain god cares for us."

"Oh, isn't that sweet. Did you hear that, dear? The mountain god watches over them."

"For crying out loud, it's a fake mountain on my map. There is no mountain god. I have people living on my fake mountain for chrissakes."

"Oh but they're not hurting anyone," she looked down at the shaman. "You're not hurting anyone, are you?"

"No ma'am. We're just trying to make a home for ourselves."

"Well, that's very commendable. I know a lot of people that would just sit around and wait for someone to come save them instead of trying to make the most of the opportunity. Good for you."

"Thank you, ma'am. It's a hard life, but we're happy with it."

"Be happy somewhere else," I barked.

"He's pretty crabby," the shaman commented.

"Oh you know how men get when they hit that age. It's all about what they have and mortality and all that. I'm just glad I was able to talk him out of buying that motorcycle."

"Yes, I used to own a motorcycle. Now we must use the indigenous llamas for transportation and honestly, ma'am, I've never felt freer."

"Please, call me Linda. This is Earl," she said, gesturing to me. "You said you had a motorcycle? Where are you from?"

"Oh we're all from Wisconsin. I'm from Green Bay originally. There are a few people from Milwaukee, a few from Osh Kosh, all over, really."

"Oh, that's so interesting. They're from Wisconsin, Earl. Isn't that where Maggie's boy is now? What was his name?"

"…Kevin," I grumbled.

"Oh, that's right. Do any of you know a Kevin? He's going to school in Madison."

"Linda, it's an entire state, not a neighborhood. Do you have any idea how many Kevin's there are in Wisconsin? Thousands, probably."

"I don't know any Kevins, but I'll ask around," the shaman offered.

"Oh, that's so sweet of you. Well, I'll leave you with Mr. Grumpy, here," she said with a wink. "It was so nice to meet you. If you guys are ever in our neck of the woods, look us up. We'll have you over for burgers."

"Thank you, I'll let the village know, Linda." With that, Linda gave a little wave and exited the office.

"Your wife's a really nice lady."

"Shut up. And pull up your loincloth. Your ass is showing."

The shaman shrugged.

"Seriously, your ass is showing."

"Why should I care? The mountain god has formed us all. I have no shame of my body."

"Then why are you wearing the loincloth?"

"Well, you know, it's a rustic area. You really don't want everything kinda flapping loose. Especially if you're clearing brush and stuff. We really don't have the best medical care up here."

"Oh God, please stop. I don't want to hear this."

The shaman shrugged.

"So there's nothing I can say to get you to leave?"

"I'm afraid not, we're pretty much gung-ho on the mountain god thing," the shaman answered apologetically.

"You guys are bastards."

"Well, I'm sorry you feel that way. For what it's worth, anytime you're in the neighborhood you're welcome to drop by for dinner or something. We'd be glad to have you."

"Patronizing sonuvabitch," I mumbled. "Listen, I'm going to give you a couple days to get your little village here moved off my map and on to somewhere else or I'm going to call my lawyer friend."

"Well, I appreciate the offer, but I think we're happy right here."

"Is there someone else down there I can talk to?"

"I'm afraid not. I'm the designated talker to gods and such. We have a chieftain, but he's more about the day-to-day administrative duties—who's hunting, who's gathering, stuff like that."

"And I can't talk to him?"

"You could, but all he'd be able to do is try and keep the noise down, enforcing noise ordinances and curfews."

"And that's it?"

"Well, there's the council of elders. We're still not sure exactly what they do. They usually talk about all the things they'd like to do and then some of the things they want to do, and some of the things they think others should do."

"And then what?"

"That's about it. They usually drink a lot and then vote and then fight and then drink some more. The council meetings are where most of our chairs get broken."

"Figures."

The shaman gave a shy shrug, "Nothing's perfect."

"Try and keep it down," I grumbled.


Have you ever read "The Tell-Tale Heart"? How the narrator hears the heart beat from beneath the floor boards even though, obviously, it's all in his head. Over the next few days I tried to ignore it but I could just hear them, their loincloths rustling across pale flabby skin as they cleared jungle brush, built little huts, hunted whatever it was that inhabited a fake mountain and, I swear to God, I heard voices singing "kum by ya" at night. Linda would say I was imagining things or that I was overreacting but I'd come home from errands there she'd be, chatting at the scribble on my map holding a magnifying glass.

That was bad enough, but soon she started telling other people about it. First it was our neighbor, Mrs. Nesbit and then some of the women in her reading group. I told her to knock it off—to stop herding people through my office and she'd just give her coy little smile and say it would all be fine and that I should just stop worrying so much.

"Dammit, I don't like people traipsing in and out of my office."

"Oh Earl, it's not like you actually *do* anything in there."

"What do you mean? I've been working on that project of mine for over a year."

"Of course you have. That's why you always come to bed smelling of brandy and there are weird long distance calls from your office line after 9pm."

"What?"

"Earl, honey, I understand you have the little things you like to play around with and you just kind of need your own personal space, but don't make it more than it is."

"It's a serious project. I've made some great progress—"

"I know, dear, but has anyone ever asked about it? I think it's nice that you're trying to keep busy, but you're really not doing anything for anybody are you?"

"That's not fair."

"I know sweetie, but we all have to come to grips with it eventually. You know Carol's husband took up golf. Have you thought about golfing? At least then you could go out with some other guys instead of being cooped up in the house all day."

"I don't want to golf."

"Well, not golf then. Cindy's husband builds those little ships inside bottles. Wouldn't that be fun?"

"No."

"Well, think about it. You should find something to do instead of complain. No one likes a grumpy Gus."

"Grumpy Gus?"

"Hush. Dinner will be ready in about a half hour. Oh, and don't bother the nice boy from the paper until he's finished."

"What?"

"They're doing a little story on the mountain people. Don't worry, they'll be done soon."

Sure enough, the next day on the front page was a blurry photo of the little tribe of survivors waving under the headline "Exploring the Mystery Tribe." Below was a smaller picture of Linda standing by the map in my office. She'd tried to get me to be in the picture, but I wanted nothing to do with it.

Apparently the story hit the news wire and had been reprinted all over. We were getting calls from all corners, from curious readers to television morning show producers to angry religious people condemning the mountain god. It didn't take long before I had all but lost my office to the steady parade of press people, well-wishers and academic types, all trying to get their peek at the Wisconites.

The last straw was when I was forced to answer questions from a sixth grade class that came by for a tour. They gathered in the living room. I had wanted to leave, but Linda made me sit with her and answer their questions. I had started drinking early that day.

"How did they get there?" asked one sandy-haired girl in the back.

"I don't know," I mumbled as I took another sip of brandy.

Linda smiled, "We're not sure how they got there, honey. One night Earl was being a little silly and drew on the map like you saw and the next day they were there."

"I was drunk."

"Hush, Earl."

Another hand shot up. "Why do they dress like that?"

"Well, you see, when you're clearing brush you don't want —"

"What Earl means is that it's very hot there and it's more comfortable for them to wear that kind of clothing."

A little red-headed kid with a runny nose interjected, "Why do they live in huts? Why don't they have houses?"

Linda smiled, "Well dear, you see different cultures have different kinds of houses. Like Eskimos in igloos or Indians in tepees—"

"Oh for Christ sakes, they're from Wisconsin. They live in huts because that's what squatters do. They move in, put up the cheapest damn buildings they can find and refuse to leave even though they have no right to be there. There are plenty of nice places in Wisconsin, I'm sure. But they had to crash on my mountain. Tom Wopat's from Wisconsin and he's done fine for himself. He doesn't need to live on my map, goddammit."

"Well, I think Earl needs to take a nap. He can get a little cranky when he's tired," Linda stammered. "Why don't you go in the back and eat your sandwiches and we'll continue the tour after lunch."

"Continue the tour? It's my office. How much can you see in my office?"

"Earl, this isn't the time or place."

"Aw Christ, I'm going to get a drink." I stomped out and headed to Bernie's.

Usually Bernie's was a nice place to relax. It catered mostly to the nine-to-five crowd—people unwinding after a long day at work, just coming for a nice drink, maybe a little conversation with a familiar face or to just be left alone.

"Hey, it's the man of the hour!" yelled Jimmy the bartender when I walked in. The smattering of patrons that were there at noon applauded. "This is the guy I told you about. The guy with the mountain people. I saw you on 'Good Morning America' this morning."

"I wasn't on the show; that was Linda."

"No, there was a second where you walked behind her in your bathrobe going to the john or something."

"Oh Jesus…"

"No, it was good. I got to tell my old lady that I finally knew someone who was on the news for something other than getting arrested."

"Great."

"Drink's on me, Earl. Not everyday we get a celebrity in here."

"I'll take a whiskey sour. Keep 'em coming."

The evening became fuzzier and fuzzier. Jimmy kept pointing me out to the regulars as the "Village People Guy" which, as far as I can recall, was misinterpreted by at least a couple patrons. The last thing I really remember was sulking in my corner, pitching back a whiskey coke and then…

"Oh my God!" Linda screamed.

I didn't know what time it was, I was on the little couch in my office (and I probably wasn't aware of that at the time) when she'd let out her yelp. My head was pounding, my mouth tasted like something had first shit in it and then curled up next to it and died. And Linda was screaming.

"What did you do?"

"What did I do about what?"

"Oh my God Earl, what have you done?"

I cracked my eyelids and saw the blurry form of Linda pointing at the map emphatically.

"What are you talking about?"

She didn't answer; she just ran out of the room crying. I didn't remember anything about the night before. I wasn't even sure how I got home, honestly. I gingerly sat up and felt my stomach shift anyway. It was clear that the last drink I remembered having wasn't, in fact, the last drink.

I got up and made my way to the map. I had hoped that I'd just thrown it away, but it was still there. At first I had no idea what she was carrying on about. It took my eyes a moment to focus and then I saw it. Next to the squiggle that designated the San Madre Punta mountain range was a strange reptilian looking creature with an arrow pointing to it that said "Chupacabra".

I picked up the magnifying glass and looked in at the little village. There were some huts burned to the ground, and patches of what looked like blood. There were a few villagers cleaning up. The shaman saw me and gave a little wave.

"Long time no see," he said.

"Well, I've been busy. I don't like cameras."

"They've been around a lot lately, haven't they? I heard there's a website about us."

"Probably."

"Well, I don't mean to be rude, but we've got some clean up to take care of."

"What happened?"

"We had an incident last night."

"Really?" I hoped I didn't sound guilty.

"Some sort of creature came into the village. We lost a few people last night. It's been a rough day."

"What kind of creature? Like a lion?"

"No, some kind of lizard thing. I've never seen anything like it before."

"That's terrible. Maybe you should all leave?" I offered hopefully.

"No, the mountain god is sending this to us as a test of our faith. The mountain god is watching over us. This creature will only prove the mountain god is protecting us."

"Protecting you by letting some of you get killed?"

176

"Well, we were kinda taking it for granted before."

"That's no answer. It could be that it's just not safe there. I mean, no one's lived on a fake mountain before; there could be all kind of things out there to get you. Like trolls and stuff."

"Well, the mountain god is bigger and stronger than all of them. If he saw fit to create them, then there must be a purpose behind it."

"Maybe the purpose was to tell you to get the hell off the mountain."

The shaman smiled. "You are a crafty one, Earl. The mountain god was right in choosing you to tempt us."

"So you're not leaving?"

"Not today."

"Tomorrow?"

"Only if the mountain god tells us to."

"So that's a no?"

"Who among us is wise enough to know the ways of the mountain god before he reveals himself?"

"So that's a no."

"Probably."

"I'm hungover. I'm going to go back to bed."

"Okay, well thanks for dropping by Earl. Don't be a stranger."

I went to lie on the couch again, trying to get back to sleep, but the guilt I felt in the pit of my stomach, combined with the liquor, refused to sit calmly. I tried to rationalize away my responsibility—it was a fake mountain being terrorized by a fake monster. It was all so stupid there's no way I could be blamed.

Or the fact that my fake mountain had a fake monster shouldn't concern anyone and if the Wisconsites thought they'd just sit and camp on it—well, they were doing so at their own risk. Or that I'd been drunk and hadn't remembered drawing the Chupacabra. Perhaps some prankster had seen it all on the news and drawn it on there while Linda slept and I was three sheets to the wind.

The worst part was that they didn't blame me. It was the mountain god's doing. And they didn't blame him, either. They should've been fighting mad. They should have been crafting weapons to track the bugger down and kill it or at least found a way off the mountain long enough to kick my wrinkled ass. But they didn't. They just buried their dead and thanked the mountain god for being worthy of being tested. Or apologized for not having been good enough not to be tested. It's so hard to tell the difference sometimes.

I sauntered into the kitchen about an hour later to find a scribbled note. Linda hadn't been too impressed with my drunken Chupacabra idea and was going to spend the next two weeks at her sister's house.  From the tone of the letter I thought she was coming back, but then again, it really didn't sound like a guarantee.

I spent the day not answering the phone and shooing away reporters and tourists from my front lawn.  By that evening speculation on the television was growing that either the village was a hoax or that something horrible had happened.

If I hadn't been so hungover, I'm pretty sure all the new attention would have driven me to drink again.  That night, as the reporters camped out on the street, I crept into the office.  I looked down on the little village.  There wasn't a sound below.  I took out my white out and covered up the Chupacabra and the sign.  Now it would at least leave the villagers alone.  I couldn't let any outsiders come by or else they'd see the crudely covered sketch by the mountain.  It was still a mess, but hopefully I'd minimized the damage.

I went to bed that night feeling confident that I was still a decent person and deserving of a good night's sleep.

I awoke feeling considerably better.  There were a few less television news vans out in front and some of the reporters had left too.  It seemed like things had finally taken a good turn.  I made some coffee and decided to check in on my little herd of squatters.

When I looked down I expected to see the villagers working and building and doing little villager things.  What I found was a massacre.  There were bodies everywhere— dismembered, disemboweled, and every possible permutation in between. The shaman was sitting in the middle of the village, head bowed, not making a sound.

"What happened?" I asked.

The shaman looked up at me. "It came back."

"It came back? Are you sure?"

"Well, not completely sure. It might have been something else. This one was invisible."

"What?"

"It came in the night and then in broad daylight. It acted and sounded like the other one, but it was invisible."

"How can that be?"

"I don't know. The mountain god has sent his judgment down upon us."

"Is there anyone else left?"

"No, just me."

"You need to get out of there."

The shaman smiled sadly at me. "Always up to your tricks, aren't you? The mountain god has chosen me to be tested above all others. I'm the one he needed to test and I will not leave until I'm told to leave."

"Listen, I was the one who made the Chupacabra. That creature was my doing. I tried to make him go away after I saw what happened. I think that's why it's invisible now."

The shaman smiled, "Then the mountain god was very wise to choose you. Even when you act out of benevolence you test us. We have shown ourselves worthy. Thank you, Earl."

"Thank you? For what? I've gotten you all killed!"

"No, no, Earl," the shaman chided. "The mountain god has used you to test us. You couldn't have killed us if you wanted to. It was only by his will that this has all happened. You had your role to play, just as we did. That's why we didn't listen to you when you told us to leave the mountain—because whether you know it or not, the mountain god is even above you and your great power."

"That makes absolutely no sense. Listen, you're a real person living on a fake mountain who's about to be a fake monster's very real lunch."

"Then so be it."

"How did someone from Green Bay get to be this stupid?"

The shaman chuckled. "How did someone like you become so powerful as to create a mountain out of nothing?"

"I didn't. It's just on this stupid map."

"Then maybe we both have our roles to play."

"Okay, so let me get this straight: the mountain god brought you to the mountain, but there is no mountain."

"Right."

"But that's okay because the mountain god doesn't need a mountain."

"Yup."

"And I am not the mountain god."

"No, you're Earl."

"I'm Earl, not the mountain god, even though I created the mountain on my map."

"Yes."

"And you know I'm not the mountain god because?"

"Because the mountain god wanted us here. He wanted us to be happy and believe in him. He loves the mountain and the people on it. You created the mountain, but you don't care about it. You don't want us to believe in you and you don't care if we're happy. You just wanted us off the mountain."

"Well, I wouldn't say I didn't care if you were happy. I just thought you should be happy somewhere else."

"Ah, but there you see the flaw. We were meant to be happy by being on the mountain. If you want us off the mountain you don't really want us happy."

"Fine, whatever. So then the mountain god, because he wants you to be happy, allows me to create the Chupacabra to come and kill you all."

"Precisely."

"That doesn't seem... odd to you?"

"Not at all, should it?"

"Since when does happiness mean mass slaughter?"

"We all have our time to go. It's the mountain god's will that our days be numbered."

"You know, talking to you is like talking to a wall."

"Well, we are on a map."

"What?"

"It was a joke, sorry."

"Seems like a strange time to be joking."

"It's the perfect time to be joking."

"Why's that?"

"Because there's nothing I can do about it."

"You could leave."

"No, I couldn't."

"Why not?"

"Because this is where I am happy."

"Waiting to be gutted by an invisible fake monster makes you happy?"

"Well, it doesn't sound as good when you put it that way."

"How am I supposed to put it?"

"I'm where the mountain god wants me. He only seeks my happiness so I am happy knowing I am doing what he wishes."

"Even if that means having your intestines ripped out by a Chupacabra?"

"Especially if that means having my intestines ripped out by a Chupacabra."

"You're a nut, you know that?"

"Maybe, but I'm a happy nut."

"I'm not going to sit and watch you get killed, you know."

"I wouldn't ask you to."

"Anything you want me to tell people for you?"

The shaman thought for a moment. "Well, tell Linda thanks for the hospitality and everyone who came to visit thanks for their interest…"

"Anything else?"

"Well, I guess I'd like to thank you Earl."

"For what?"

"For being the nicest Devil there ever was. Take care, okay? And try to ease up on the drinking. You worry Linda something fierce."

With that, the shaman stood and headed into the jungle. I waited a while and then took the tacks from the corners of the map and folded it. I took out my old lighter and lit the map and set it in a metal waste paper basket that I had by my desk. I got dressed and went out the front door. There was only one reporter who noticed me.

"Is there any word from the mountain?" he asked with disinterest.

"Yeah, God help us all," I answered.

## A Fairy Tale

Once upon a time there was an old man. At least that's what reason would dictate because one cold winter morning the villagers came out of their houses to find the body of an old man. Since corpses of old men necessarily come from once living old men it was safe to assume that there had, in fact, at one time been an old man.

No one knew who he was or where he had come from. They couldn't even say for certain how long he had been dead or been dead in their town. He had been noticed one day, sitting on a park bench, eyes closed and a sad, half-smile on his face.

When the baker's wife had made the discovery she hadn't known what to do, so she simply continued with her errands and didn't mention it to anyone hoping someone else would take care of it. It wasn't until a couple of days later when she was making her way through the park again that she saw that the old man was still there. Since no one else had bothered to take care of the body she thought it was her civic duty to mention it. Perched all over him were pigeons resting between flights and feedings.

The baker's wife went to the local constable and alerted him to the situation. When they returned they found some boys hanging on him and committing acts of mischief with the corpse. Above the scene the pigeons warbled irritably that their spot was being desecrated.

The constable was unsure of how to proceed so he contacted the mayor of the village and after a lengthy discussion it was determined that a town meeting would have to be called to determine what course of action should be taken. Two weeks later the town convened at the town hall to discuss the matter.

It was soon discovered that more information would have to be gathered before the denizens of the hamlet could make a meaningful decision on the matter. A committee was called to research the matter and report back a month later to the town assembly.

The committee members first sat down and had to assign roles for the various appointed citizenry—chairman, secretary, member at large, parliamentarian, etc. After two weeks of campaigning and internal strife everything was settled and in a surprise move, Mr. Donovan, the banker was usurped as chairman and was forced to accept a position as treasurer. It was determined that the committee would first have to determine the outside effects of the dead man on the community. The committee members were dispatched to various sub-districts of the town to discuss with their constituencies the impact the old man had on their day-to-day lives, their thoughts on what should be done, as well as whether the town should accept liability for the dead man. It was also rumored Mr. Donovan was circulating a petition to have Mrs. Waterson, the committee chairman, removed from her position due to a conflict of interest since her husband was the town mortician.

The committee members found that the dead man was an unpleasant topic to discuss publicly, but more or less left the populace unaffected. Some of the more practical folk pointed out that while there would be little to no immediate impact resulting from the dead man's presence, surely by the first thaw things would change significantly. As for thoughts on what should be done, there was no consensus other than no one was particularly interested in having to pay for it. As such the town role was to be as minimal as possible. They also felt that, in response to Mrs. Waterson's survey that Mr. Donovan was far too busy with his work at the bank to oversee a committee.

The committee drafted its report and presented it to the town fathers at the monthly meeting. The local leaders thanked the committee and opted to postpone a vote on the issue until the committee's report could be fully reviewed and options discussed. The meeting was adjourned after a discussion involving a censure of Mrs. Waterson was tabled.

The old man sat, still frozen and dead on the park bench. After the first few weeks his novelty had worn off and the local children no longer felt compelled to molest the body. Since it was winter, there really was no regular traffic through the park anyway. Aside from the occasional dog walker, the old man was left alone with the pigeons that perched on his frozen arms, legs and head cooing and just generally carrying on their day-to-day pigeon duties.

The next town meeting had to be cancelled due to inclement weather and, by the time the next meeting began to roll around, the spring thaw was threatening to take up residence. The city fathers made their way through the various matters of pressing business—including Rev. Williams', the member-at-large, call to have both Mrs. Waterson and Mr. Donovan removed from the committee and he be named interim chair—and fiscal matters that had been postponed for a month and then found themselves forced to make a decision.

The city fathers noted publicly that, while the committee's report had been thorough and complete, they still felt as if they didn't have enough information to make a judgment. While the old man was clearly on city property, it could not be proven that he had expired on public property. As such, it would be ill-advised to pay for any kind of burial or removal because it could clearly be the responsibility of a private party to provide for such expenses.

On the other hand, no private party had stepped forward to acknowledge the old man. The committee had been unable to determine any kind of identity and there was no family to contact to take care of the issue. In such cases it seemed to be up to the community to determine a fair and equitable means of dealing with the old man's body. However, no one in the community knew the old man and, as a result, it would be unfair for the population at large to be shouldered with the responsibility. Unfortunately, there was no other community claiming him and a number of other local towns had refused to take ownership of him, and denying any knowledge of his identity. Mr. Donovan's suggestion that the Rev. Williams shut his mouth, accept his position on the committee or bury the old man in his own backyard was dismissed.

The city council didn't know what more could be done. However, with the spring creeping quickly over the countryside, some sort of action would have to be taken. The costs of disposing the body were discussed but rejected for being too expensive. Finally the town engineer had an idea. A bag of cement had only been partially used the previous fall for a pathway. The engineer suggested that the remainder of the cement could be mixed up and poured over the body, preventing the unfortunate results of the spring thaw from being inconvenient to the townspeople. What was more, since the body could stay where it was, should someone come through who recognized the man— who would then be both preserved and on permanent display—they could be then compelled to do their Christian duty and remove the man and return him to wherever it was he had originated. The cost of the cement as well as any other minimal fees could be extracted from them to cover the city's expense in the matter. Everyone thought the idea was absolutely grand and everyone praised the engineer for his ingenuity. The city fathers were so happy with the engineer's solution they demoted Mr. Donovan post-haste, made the engineer chairman (over the strenuous objections of the Rev. Williams and Mrs. Waterson who were subsequently censured) offered him a commendation and happily moved on to maintenance of the community swimming pool. The old man was sealed in the cement and left on the bench for all to see. And all the townspeople lived happily ever after.

The old man sat encased in cement. No one ever claimed him and the townspeople forgot about the entire situation and looked at the cement man as another decoration in the park like the lovely fountain by the stream or the picnic grounds. And the pigeons were forever content. They cooed reverently about him and told their baby pigeons about the old man with the sad smile who had died on the park bench so he could be used as a perch and shat upon by pigeons until the end of time. And the pigeons lived happily ever after, too.

The End.

*Other books by the author:*

**All Things Right and Beautiful**

**All the Lights That Have Shone**